CW01084404

LOST IN DESIRE

A LESBIAN ROMANCE

GRACE PARKES

Naomi Lawson felt a rush of fear as her phone began to vibrate in her bedroom. Minutes ago, she had ended a call with her newest client, securing an initial appointment. Now that her phone was buzzing, she feared that the woman was calling to cancel or postpone the appointment. It had happened to her multiple times since a new business rival, Squeaky Cleans, had come to town. A cancellation was the last thing she needed at this time when she was struggling to get her business going. She needed to work on getting a contract with this client. Any delay would be terrible news.

She set the duster in her hands onto the vinyl floor and hurried into the bedroom to answer the call. The phone was still buzzing when she entered the room. The fear of having her appointment canceled kept growing as she got closer to answering.

She approached the bedside and peered at the caller ID on the screen to see that it was just Jerry calling. Jerry was her undergrad younger brother who only remembered to call her when something was wrong with his laptop, and he needed extra money. He was always too swamped with coding most of the time to maintain relationships.

"Jerry, how are you?" Naomi said.

"I'm fine. How are you, and how's business?"

"Oh, it's going well," she replied. *If I don't lose this new client.*

She was unsure where this idea of her latest client going back on their agreement for an initial meeting was coming from, but she found it hard to get the thought out of her head. It likely stemmed from the scary truth that running her own business was very risky. Especially with too many new startups undercutting her prices while providing little to no effort.

"That's great to hear," Jerry said. "Have you spoken with Dad recently?"

"No, I don't think so," Naomi drew out her sentence as she tried to remember the last time she spoke with her father. They didn't really talk much because he disapproved of Naomi's decision to start working immediately after high school. He wanted her to go to college and get a *real career.*

"Well, you should call him or something, don't you think?"

Naomi rolled her eyes. She had a lot on her plate at the moment without worrying about her father, who still could not wrap his head around the fact that she had chosen not to study for another four years. Their relationship had been frosty for years, and Naomi figured things might remain that way for much longer if her father did not quit acting like she had to do everything that he wanted.

"We'll talk when we need to," Naomi said in a definitive tone. Jerry stayed on the phone for a few more minutes to talk about a coding club he just joined at his school. She could hear the excitement in his voice as he spoke about programming. It was the same passionate love that she had for cleaning. The pleasure she reaped from making something shine gave her joy every time.

Jerry hung up after saying goodbye and pleading with her again to call their dad. Naomi heaved a sigh as she slipped her phone into the pocket of her shorts. Her family wasn't the cutest in the world, and her life was not exactly rosy, but her love for cleaning was one of the things that kept her going. Maybe the only thing, to be frank. The smell of a freshly scrubbed house was everything to Naomi, and getting paid to do what she loved was just awesome. It was the way she lived, the way she paid the bills, and the way she kept her life afloat.

She turned away from the bed and headed toward the door to resume decluttering and deep cleaning her living room. On her way out of the room, her eyes caught the reflection of her body in the mirror on the wall, and she turned to take a better look. Her dark hair was disheveled, and her pretty, round face had a smile on it. Her world was on the edge of financially crumbling, but that smile was always on her face. She flexed the muscles of her bare arms, and her smile grew wider. She was proud of her nicely toned arms and her slightly athletic build. It was the product of years of discipline with clean eating and regular exercise, and she liked to show those arms off when she could.

Naomi took her eyes off of the mirror and walked back to the living room. She had set a part of that room aside for her business. It was a one-woman business, but Naomi was juggling everything quite well. The only thing that could be better was if she had a few more clients at the moment. Some of her old clients had decided to stop using her services, preferring to get on board with a medium-sized cleaning firm that had just opened in town. Some of them were just plain mean to her even though she did her work with extreme diligence. Her prices were a little higher, but they reflected the quality of her work.

With half an hour left before she had to get changed and head to her afternoon appointment, she picked up the hand duster off the floor and started dusting the top of her drawers. Today she had Sally Cohen's house to clean. She was grateful to Sally for her customer loyalty and for recommending her to Miss Smithson, her new client with whom she had just secured an initial appointment, right after Sally's. That would go a long way in sustaining her business while remaining on the lookout for more customers. She only hoped that between now and the time she would meet the woman that Squeaky Cleans would not have snatched her away. As Naomi checked her cleaning cart, her eyes ran over the mop, the vacuum, and everything else she may need. When she had confirmed that everything was in place, she headed back to her room to put her hair in order and dress for the trip to Sally's house.

BEFORE SHE KNEW IT, it was time to meet Miss Smithson, and Naomi was absolutely determined to make a good impression on her. Her passion for making her business work had recently caused extra anxiety, making her hands feel surprisingly clammy as she turned on the ignition.

After checking her face in the mirror, she took several deep breaths as she drove the rest of the way to Miss Smithson's house. She remembered the uneasiness that she had struggled with when Miss Smithson called her for the first time. The woman sounded so relaxed and self-assured—everything Naomi wanted to be and more—and Naomi had been thrown off balance by the fear of losing a potential client and the uncertainty of working for someone so sophisticated. She admired confidence but struggled to obtain it.

She took one last peek at her reflection in the rear mirror as her car pulled up outside the vast property. Her dark hair was in a bun, and her face carried its usual smile that masked all of her problems quite nicely. When she was satisfied with what she saw, she opened the door and stepped out of the car, drawing floral-scented air into her nose. It was late afternoon, and the sun stood out clearly in the blue sky. Naomi thought of herself living in such an affluent neighborhood where the air was fragrant, and buildings were larger and more beautiful.

"I'll get there one day," she whispered to herself as she walked over to the trunk of her car. She was about to open it when she remembered that she was not there to clean, at least not yet. She was to meet her client in person for the first time and talk about anything that needed to be sorted out. It looked like the woman preferred to pay fixed prices for cleaning, but Naomi wanted to get paid by the hour. They had to talk about that too.

After realizing that she didn't need her equipment or supplies on this occasion, she turned away from her car and headed straight to the front door of her new client's house. Her footsteps were brisk as she made her way to Miss Smithson's door. She slipped her hands into the pockets of her denim pants as she tried to keep her uneasiness out of her head. She wondered why she felt squidgy inside. She had been in this business for too long. She was not alien to meeting different kinds of people, but on this occasion, Naomi struggled to get her nerves together. Maybe it was the make-or-break nature of this business deal that made her this way. *It had to be.*

She reached the front entrance and delivered a quick knock on the beautifully crafted wooden door.

"Just a moment, please," a voice from inside the house floated into Naomi's ears.

Naomi clenched her fist as she waited for Miss Smithson to open the door. The door swung open, and as Naomi looked up, she saw the most striking pair of eyes that she had ever come across. Those blue eyes were peering right back at her, but they were not hostile in any way. Miss Smithson was a beautiful blonde with a curvy body, and Naomi quickly guessed her age as early forties. Damn it, Naomi thought, she's stunning.

"Hello, Miss Smithson, I'm..."

"Naomi," Miss Smithson said with a smile across her face, "please, come in. And please call me Tanya."

Tanya ushered Naomi into the house. She did her best not to appear wide-eyed at the beauty of the interior. It was like something out of a glamorous movie. Naomi tried to imagine herself pushing the vacuum on the fancy flooring as she stood in Tanya's living room.

"Please, sit," Tanya said. "Do you mind if I take a few minutes to answer some really urgent messages? I'll be with you as quickly as possible."

"No, I don't mind," Naomi said, although she thought it was possible for Tanya to work on the messages while they discussed the contract. But it was her house, and she was the one giving Naomi the job, so she could do as she damned well pleased.

"Thank you. I'll be with you shortly," Tanya said, and Naomi thought she saw the woman wink at her. Did her eye muscles just happen to twitch when she was about to excuse herself? Naomi couldn't be sure.

Naomi found herself staring at Tanya's curvy figure as she gracefully walked out of the living room. It was the kind of body she would have loved to have if she wasn't such a fitness freak. She took her eyes off Tanya's backside and let them wander around the living room. It was clear that Tanya Smithson was just as Sally had described her —a thriving businesswoman with a loving personality. What Sally had omitted was that Tanya was an absolute beauty, having the kind of face that could grace the screens of Hollywood films. For some reason, the fear of losing Tanya's business to Squeaky Cleans returned to her head again. Now that she knew how warm and welcoming Tanya's personality was, Naomi was desperate to work for her. She hoped this first meeting would end up with a signed deal.

2

Tanya lingered a moment at the door as she watched her new cleaner hop into her old, red Fiat. Their discussion about the cleaning schedule had gone really well. Tanya had no reservations about Naomi's character, having already been told that she was professional and really hard working. She had come across as shy in the opening minutes of their exchange, but Tanya had taken it upon herself to make Naomi feel at ease. Tanya realized that Naomi took her business seriously but could laugh just as hard when she relaxed a bit.

The car had turned onto the road now, so Tanya stepped back into her house. It would take a while to get the image of Naomi's toned arms out of her head. Tanya had felt the urge to reach out and run her hands down those powerful arms, but she didn't do it because she wasn't sure Naomi would be comfortable with that. Heck, it had taken a bit of little banter for her to look relatively at ease. Touching her like that would surely scare her away... or would it?

Tanya didn't want to put that to the test. It didn't feel right to take such bold steps amid a potential business deal. She wanted this dark-haired hottie coming into her house twice every week, and she would do well to keep her hands to herself. She could not remember a time when she had been so captivated by a complete stranger. Another issue was that Naomi gave off zero gay vibes. Tanya was pretty good at figuring out if a woman was into other women and enjoyed spontaneous, casual fucking. Naomi did remind Tanya of her first love affair decades ago when she was in college. Selena had been a terrific switch. She was as generous with giving pleasure as she was in being responsive to the sensual touches of her partner.

Thinking about Selena turned Tanya on, making her itch for a bit of time alone with her thoughts. Thoughts of Selena's thighs around her back as she fucked her to the edge of pleasure were making Tanya horny as hell. She would have loved to hurry into her bedroom, shed her shirt, kick off her skirt, and pleasure herself, but she could not do that at the moment. She needed to prepare for a meeting with Freddy, one of her business partners. She simply did not have that kind of spare time, hence the need to hire Naomi to take care of domestic matters.

Freddy was a difficult man. He was one of those men who believed that a good *dicking* could make a lesbian change her sexual preference. A term that made Tanya want to vomit. He had never really stopped staring at her ever since they had gone into business together. He was handsome and rich, and he believed that those qualities would entice every lady into his bed. Still, Tanya didn't care about his looks or the depth of his pockets. She just wasn't into men, and she had never been. She had been lucky to discover her sexuality long ago in middle school, allowing her years of exploring everything she desired.

Naomi is such a beautiful woman, Tanya mused to herself as she pulled on a jacket over her shirt. It was clear that she was going to have Naomi in her head for days to come. She admires the body structure of the kind cleaner and her pretty face.

I guess everybody has the potential to be a little gay, Tanya thought before realizing she needed to keep her cool. She could not cross business with pleasure, and she couldn't scare the poor girl away with her fleeting desires. Tanya just loved women. She equally loved fucking them.

Tanya grabbed her keys and headed straight to the door. She locked up and walked to her garage to get in her car. The meeting with Freddy wasn't too far off, and she hated nothing more than having someone wait for her when it came to business. She had not become the big boss of an artist management company by being a slouch. A lot of hard work had gone into building the company, and the journey had not been easy. But Tanya had stuck her foot in, and now her efforts had begun to pay off. She could afford to live grander, drive more expensive rides and live in a more refined side of the city, but she never forgot where she had come from. Growing up in a poor town with her mom installed good values and a drive to make something of her life.

Tanya got in her car and started the engine. She could make it to the office in a few minutes, just in time to catch up with her associate. She braced herself for more remarks from Freddy about how hot she looked or how he liked the color of today's lipstick. He would never give up on trying to charm her into his bed, no matter how many times she told him that going out with men was not her cup of tea. The problem was, she couldn't get rid of the letch just yet, not until she had a plan in place. She knew that it would cause a whole mess of issues if she wasn't careful, even though it should never be so difficult.

A glance at her watch showed that she would be late if she didn't hit the gas. That meeting with Naomi had taken longer than she scheduled for, and that was probably why she was running late. Tanya had zero regrets because she didn't mind sitting there, staring into Naomi's chestnut eyes. Tanya could not understand why she was so attracted to her. It felt more profound than just liking her physical outlook, and it had come out of nowhere. She had no time to process it because she had to keep her mind on business right now. When she had cleared everything on her schedule for the day, then she could return home and think about Naomi Lawson and maybe indulge herself in those thoughts.

Maybe I should call Peggy. Tanya edged the car onto the road and began to drive in the direction of the office where she and Freddy were to hold their meeting. She and Freddy had agreed that physical meetings worked better for them when it came to certain aspects of their business than other options like corresponding over email or talking over the phone. Tanya kept her hands on the steering wheel as she tried to blank out the intruding image of Naomi's toned arms and lean body from her mind. She found herself looking forward to the next visit by the cleaner. Three days had never felt so far away for Tanya Smithson.

TANYA CLOSED her eyes as she felt the cold jab of water against her naked body after she turned on the shower. She had decided to wash off the stickiness of her skin after the busy day that she had. After the meeting with Freddy, one thing led to another, and she had become lost in a world of work, work, and more work. Tanya took a deep breath as she felt the continuous touch of the cool water on her skin. Finally, she felt refreshed. Her eyes were no longer heavy with sleep, and all the tiredness in her bones had eased away with the water that had run down her skin. She toweled the moisture away and stepped out of the bathroom. There were times when she felt lonely in this house and when she wished there was someone to meet when she returned from home—a girl to talk to about the day's work, a girl to kiss and cuddle...

These lonely thoughts only occurred occasionally. Tanya had a pretty busy life, and most times, she returned from work too tired to think about anything. On days like this, when she could get herself to take a cold shower, she would be active for about an hour, either watching music channels on TV or having one of those long conversations with her sister, Aliana, on the phone before going to bed. Today, she didn't feel like sitting in front of the TV to watch *Pristine Voices*. She wanted to fall into her bed and start again tomorrow.

Tanya walked into her bedroom and flicked off the light, leaving the bedside lamp as the only source of illumination in the room. She rubbed her eyes and walked over to the window to observe the moon as it peeked from behind the dark evening clouds. She wasn't going to call her sister today. They had spoken at length about two days ago, and it would be about a week before they would have many things to talk about again. There were times when Tanya wished her life was as simple as her sister's. Aliana was already married, and they had adopted two dark-haired girls. Aliana lived in a neighboring small town with her sweetheart, and she maintained close contact with their mother, who was their only surviving parent.

Tanya kept her eyes on the moon as she wondered if she should visit the gay club in the city to try and meet some new people, maybe arrange a hook-up. She had already been told about the Rainbow Bar, and she felt it might just be the solution to all the boredom that had plagued her recently, even before she moved into this new area.

Rainbow Bar was such a dumb name. Couldn't they be a little more inventive? Tanya thought to herself as she stared into the sky. Her house was so big and so empty, sometimes she felt so lonely, but a smile appeared on her face as she fantasized about bumping into Naomi at the Rainbow Bar.

"Fat chance of that," Tanya chuckled. She knew Naomi wasn't gay. The chances of seeing her in a lesbian club were pretty slim.

With a deep sigh, Tanya dragged her eyes off the moon and walked to her bed. Using the bedside lamp, she reached for the little drawer on the big stool that stood next to her bed, and she took out her vibrating wand. She sucked her lips in anticipation of the rush of pleasure that she was about to feel.

3

Naomi got off her knees as she turned off the vacuum and took a look around the living room. It was squeaky clean, and she admired her hard work. She was proud of her achievement and satisfied that she had done enough to keep Miss Smithson impressed. The scent of the cleaning products she used tingled in her nostrils as she walked away from the room to tell her employer that it was time for her to leave. Naomi liked to use non-toxic cleaning products—another unique selling point she was proud of.

"Miss Smi... Umm, Tanya, I'm done," Naomi was still not used to calling her by her first name. It had been three weeks of smooth sailing with the job, yet she struggled to get comfortable with the other woman.

"It's Tanya, dammit," Naomi said under her breath. Naomi heard something that sounded like a cry from one of the bedrooms. She instantly became alarmed. Was Tanya in danger? Was she in pain or something?

Tanya had returned from work not long ago. Feeling a rush of fear and a sense of duty to try and help Tanya if she was in trouble, Naomi rushed towards the room where she thought the shout came from. Her heart was beating fast as she approached the door, wondering what exactly could have gone wrong. Hundreds of thoughts were bouncing wildly in her head as she hurried towards the room. When she got close to the door, she heard the sound again, clearer this time, and she realized that it was a moan. It sounded like Tanya was watching some sleazy stuff in her room.

"Tanya, I'm..." Naomi called as she saw Tanya on the other side of the door, getting dressed, revealing one of her breasts. The wide areola drew Naomi's attention as well as the fullness of Tanya's breast. She stared unashamedly for a moment before she took her eyes away abruptly.

"Oh," Tanya said casually as if it didn't matter that Naomi had just seen her getting dressed. Tanya really wasn't fazed by much.

"I'm sorry," Naomi muttered. She had only tried to help, not knowing that she would get herself into this awkward situation.

"It's nothing. Don't worry about it." Tanya put her offending breast back inside her bra and pulled down her cream-colored shirt, yet Naomi still struggled to get the image of that dusty rose areola out of her head. "You liked what you saw, didn't you?" Tanya said with a smirk on her face.

Naomi was not sure what stunned her more, Tanya's question or the tiny wink that had followed it. Over the few weeks that she had been working here, she had had her suspicions that Tanya was into girls, and now she had her confirmation.

"I, uh... I'll leave now," Naomi said. She could not

bring herself to tell Tanya that she liked seeing her full breast or that she felt like placing a kiss on her nipple followed by getting to know more of her body. It was all too crazy for her to think about. What was it about Tanya that made Naomi so attracted to her?

"Okay, I understand. I'm not mad that you caught me with a boob out. It's not like you haven't seen one before. Don't worry, okay?"

"Yeah," Naomi said. It was a little difficult for her to look at Tanya's face. She was still unsettled by what she had seen. Something had shifted within Naomi, and she needed to process it far away from this gorgeous woman because she simply couldn't understand what her feelings were anymore. It was a good thing that she had finished her work for the day already. She could not imagine having to work in the house now with Tanya still around, watching her as she liked to.

Tanya nodded and smiled as she put on her jacket. There was something about the way that their eyes locked that filled the room with a certain ambiance. Was it really just a desire for friendship or something even deeper?

Naomi grabbed her bag and headed straight for the door, saying goodbye to her employer as she hurried out of the house. Once she stepped out of Tanya's house, she let out a deep breath. She needed to sit in her car for a while and just think about everything that had happened. She was beginning to question so many things about herself now, and she wanted to understand the attraction she had for Tanya. It looked like it was way deeper than a girl admiring an older, more successful woman, more than being in awe of her oozing confidence.

She got to her car and headed to the trunk to store her equipment. Her eyes strayed back to Tanya's house, and she was surprised to see her standing at the door, looking at her. From the considerable distance, Naomi could see the gentle smile on her employer's face, like that of a proud parent watching her kid do something nice.

This is supposed to be creepy. But, in a way, she enjoyed the attention that she got from Tanya. Naomi waved at her and hurried to get into the car. Now, she could not sit behind the wheel and think about what was happening. She had to drive away, maybe go back to her house, although she didn't feel like it at the moment. In her head, she did a quick survey of the places she could go to, and she found that her choices were pretty limited. Outside the houses she cleaned, Naomi didn't have any place that she frequented. Maybe this was the time to try out the bar that she had seen around the streets. *I could do with a drink.*

She tried to think back to the last time she had enjoyed the attention of another woman like this, and she couldn't really recall any particular instance. Now that Tanya wasn't watching her, Naomi started replaying the events of the evening in her head. She wished she had known that Tanya was not in trouble when she had heard that shout, then she would not have been close to her bedroom. And she would not have seen her change clothes. It felt as if the image of Tanya's breast and soft skin were fixed in her mind, and it would take some time before she would forget about it. She didn't want to forget about it, did she?

God, I hope it's not awkward when I next go over, Naomi thought, letting out a sigh. All she could hope for was that it would be one of those days when her client would not be at home. Naomi usually cleaned the house when Tanya was busy with work or some other stuff, but

there were days when she would be there while Naomi
was cleaning, and she liked to talk about random things
with her. Naomi knew it was all to make her feel more
comfortable while she did her work.

"Let's go to the bar, baby," Naomi whispered to the
rearview mirror. She realized at that point that she had
not yet taken off her cleaning apron. She thought of
walking into the bar in this blue apron but figured it
would make people wonder what was going on with her.
The last thing she wanted was that kind of attention.

What kind of attention do you want anyway?

Naomi shook her head. She wasn't ready for this
mental debate about whether she liked the way Tanya
Smithson looked at her or not. For now, she only wanted
to do something she had not done in a long, long time—
head to a bar and just socialize until it was dark. Then she
would go back home and sleep it off.

NAOMI LISTENED to the guy seated next to her at the bar,
talking about his IT business and how technology was
progressing at a faster rate in this era. She sat through his
talk while sipping her glass of shandy. She had opted for a
drink that would not get her drunk because she had to
drive back home.

Surprisingly, the bar didn't have many customers in it
that night. The bartender looked bored standing behind
the bar, stifling a yawn every now and then. Naomi
wondered if the bar usually had low patronage like this or
if it was just today. She tapped the side of her glass with
her fingers as the words of the dude seated next to her
floated past her ears. He had told her his name, but

Naomi had forgotten it already. She really didn't find him interesting, and she would have loved to spend her time listening to someone else, but with the low numbers in the bar, her options were pretty limited.

"So, what do you do?" he asked her, trying to bring her into the conversation for the first time.

"Cleaning business," she replied.

"Do you work with Pro Cleaners or Squeaky Cleans?"

"Nah, I run my own cleaning outfit," she replied as she wondered when Pro Cleaners had come to town. Why were these firms springing up like every day? She hoped that none of her clients would be swayed to dump her and register with those big cleaning businesses.

"That's impressive," the guy said. "I have a cousin who runs a similar business in Sacramento. He has been doing it for years, and he has become really successful at it…"

Naomi peered at him as he droned on about his cousin. She was studying his freshly cut and well-trimmed beard. Maybe she would have liked to hang out with him more if he talked less and listened more. She knew that it could be his drink that was making it difficult to keep his words in.

"Errr, excuse me for a moment," Naomi said as she got up from her seat. She knew she was not coming back to this man. Before she walked away from the bar, she drained her glass of shandy, enjoying that taste of lemonade mixed with beer. After that, she paid for the drink and tipped the bartender.

"Hey Naomi, are you leaving already?" the guy called out as she began to move away from the bar.

What does it look like? Naomi didn't respond to the guy's query. The fact that his name had gone over her head showed how much interest she had in his company. The laughter and conversations of the few people in the bar mixed with the background of soft music filled her ears as she walked out of the bar. Between chatting with the bartender and listening to the monotone voice of the chatty guy who sat next to her as soon as she had, Naomi had managed to get Tanya and the awkward moment out of her head. Now that she was heading back home, she feared that she would get caught again in the web of unwanted attraction that she felt towards Tanya.

The night wind felt warm against the skin of her exposed forearm. She wished for a while that she had hooked up with some guy at the bar. The kind of guy that she liked and not someone who was going to bore the life out of her with needless talking. Naomi cracked her knuckles as she walked to her car. She hadn't had sex since she split with her ex, Jack, and there were days when she felt that longing for some warmth in her bed. She had gotten close to hooking up with a guy she met when she had visited a local art gallery, but nothing had come out of it in the end. It had been three years since she split with Jack, three long years without sex.

Naomi adjusted her flowing hair as she approached her old car. She had to do something about her sexless life pretty soon. She had been focusing all of her energy on her business, but it was time to take a step back and get laid. *It's been so long.*

It didn't matter that Squeaky Cleans and, now, Pro Cleaners were putting pressure on her small business. She had her clients, and she knew that she would get more people. There were enough people around to work with. She needed to stop worrying about other people's business.

4

The week had gone nicely, Naomi thought as she scrubbed the floor of Sally's house. She had managed to add two more clients to her list of customers, and she had earned enough to buy more goods for her business. The idea of employing someone to work with her was already taking shape in her head. She was already getting close to the point where she could not handle all her clients alone.

Even better was the fact that she was getting close to Seth, the son of her latest client. Seth was a bodybuilder, and he played on the local baseball team. They had started talking when Seth returned from training and found her cleaning his mom's house. Naomi had found that Seth was the kind of guy she liked to be around and maybe have sex with. There was a bit of a connection, but they were still at the early stages of their friendship, so she wasn't sure about anything yet. She also wasn't sure if maybe her lack of sexual contact was driving her crazy.

Naomi got off her knees as she ran her eyes over the area she had just cleaned. She saw a patch that was still unclean, so she immediately attacked it with her brush. After cleaning the floors, her next port of call would be Mrs. Cohen's bathroom. That was the most tasking part of her work, but she didn't mind cleaning anywhere or anything, from dirty bathroom tiles to stained toilet seats. That was what she was paid to do. Naomi kept working on the living room floor until she had removed every bit of the stain. Then she took off her gloves and sat on the chair for a brief rest. Her eyes flicked to the black and white pictures on the staircase wall. Sally and her husband were holding hands and smiling. Naomi thought about what her own family frame would look like, maybe with a fair-haired guy and one or two kids.

"Get to work, Naomi. Stop dreaming," she told herself.

She got off of the chair and went to grab the squeegee and toilet brushes from her bag. It was amusing that when she thought of the fair-haired guy in her family picture, her mind had flickered to Tanya. Naomi had managed to overcome the initial awkwardness that followed seeing Tanya when she was dressing. She was grateful that the unfortunate moment had not ruined the professional relationship with the woman. Tanya wasn't bothered whatsoever, so it was just Naomi's insecurities and confusion causing her to worry about everything. A certain level of anxiety was following her around more than usual lately.

Naomi was walking towards the bathroom when she heard the sound of the door being opened. She halted and turned to see who it was.

"Hey, Naomi," Sally said as she came through the door. She had two grocery bags in her hands, and she looked like she could do with a bit of rest.

Naomi offered to help with one of the bags, but Sally

told her not to bother. She asked Naomi how the work was going.

"Almost done. Only the bathroom is left," Naomi said.

"Ah, you should get to it."

"Yeah, right away."

Naomi took her supplies and headed to the bathroom. It wasn't in a terrible state, but it was still going to take some time to make it sparkling clean like everything else she had cleaned in the house. She adjusted the gloves on her hands and got ready for the tough business ahead.

Now that Sally was back, the relative silence in the house disappeared. The sound of her heavy footsteps on the floor and the meows of the family cat that only came out of hiding when Sally filled the house everywhere. The TV soon came on and, Naomi could hear the commentary of a sports event, most likely basketball, from the bathroom where she had already begun to clear clumps of hair from the shower drain.

As Naomi worked on the bathroom, she thought about hanging out with Seth later in the evening. That would be possible if he didn't have a training session fixed for that period. Her hopes of getting laid rested on Seth, for now at least. She didn't have the time and energy to invest in a full-blown relationship, but she could put up with a friendship that involved no-strings-attached sex. She was sure Seth would love the idea. She had learned early in her life that most guys would not pass up a chance to go to bed with a willing female, especially when the situation didn't necessitate commitment.

There was a part of her that didn't want Seth, though. That part was still enchanted by Tanya's gorgeous body and her kind nature. Naomi didn't understand why her admiration for Tanya seemed to be interfering with her friendship with Seth. She was left wondering if she was romantically attracted to Tanya, which led her to question her sexuality and choice of partners so far. Naomi kept a firm grip on the squeegee as she continued with her cleaning. She decided to focus all of her attention on the cleaning that she had to do. Later, she would have the time to ponder the Seth versus Tanya debate in her head.

TANYA STRETCHED her arms after ending her meeting with her business partners at her company's main office. She was famished and had decided that she would grab a snack on her way back home. She didn't like eating out unless it was a special occasion or she had a date with someone. She loved the idea of making her own dishes whenever she wasn't too tired from work. She thought of her house, knowing that Naomi would have cleaned everywhere and would have left already. Tanya wished that Naomi would still be cleaning when she got back, but that was unlikely. She only got to see Naomi on days that she finished work early. Their friendship had grown stronger in many ways, although Tanya doubted if Naomi ever saw her as a friend. She always had that look of awe whenever she was around Tanya as if there was something about Tanya that she could only dream of having.

"Kate," Tanya dialed up her secretary before leaving, "send the Logan reports to my email."

"Alright, ma'am," Kate replied.

Shortly after that, Tanya grabbed her bag and strutted out of her office. On her way out of the office complex, she saw some young people auditioning for the company's program for musical talent in the surrounding areas. She saw hope in their faces, and she silently wished them the best. Tanya had always loved anything creative, and her dream was to give people chances to achieve their dreams too.

She stepped outside to see Freddy approaching the door. His lips expanded into a wide smile as he came closer to her. He had not been talking to her about them growing a special friendship anymore. Since a little accident that had involved his child, the man had been paying more attention to his family. Or had he just found another woman to turn his attention to?

"Hey, Freddie."

"Lady Tanya," Freddy smiled wider. "You didn't leave early today?"

"I was meeting with Aarons and Logan,' Tanya told him. "You forget stuff in the office?"

"Yeah," Freddy said.

"Okay, go get your stuff. I'll be on my way now."

Tanya walked away from Freddy toward the parking lot where she had parked her car. She could not wait to grab a quick bite before getting home to whip up something more substantial in the kitchen. She wasn't sure what to cook yet, but she would make that decision before she got back home.

Tanya was about to get in her car when her phone rang. She quickly took it out and checked the caller ID. It was her sister, Aliana. Tanya remembered that it had been a long while since she and her sister talked last. She got in the car first before answering the call and turned on the hands-free option.

"Hey, Ana. How are you doing?" Tanya said the moment she answered the call.

She didn't get a response from her sister, only something that sounded like sniffs in the background.

"What's wrong, Ana? Talk to me!" Tanya shrieked. She began to think of a host of things that could have been wrong with her sister. None of the things she thought about were good. "Come on, tell me what is going on."

"Mum's sick. It's critical," Aliana managed to say before she broke into tears.

Tanya was confused. Aliana wasn't one to break down so quickly, so she knew it was bad.

"Oh, goodness," Tanya muttered. "Where's she now?"

"Harriet and I are taking her to the hospital, but I'm scared, Tanya. She looks so pale," Aliana said.

Tanya took in a sharp breath as she gripped the steering wheel tightly. "I'll be there with you as quickly as I can make it."

Aliana continued to sob on the phone. Tanya tried her best to calm her before needing to end the call and set herself in the opposite direction. She had to get to her mother as quickly as possible.

5

Naomi was excited to clean at Tanya's house. She received a text from her two days ago that she was back in town after vising her sick mother in a neighboring town. When Tanya had been away, Naomi had found that she missed her so much. She had somehow grown used to hearing Tanya talk to her about girly things after she was done with the cleaning. She truly missed seeing Tanya's attractive face and the beautiful smile that was always on it.

The air smelled fresh as Naomi stepped out of her car. She had been around once to clean Tanya's house when she was away. The interior of the house had felt different on that occasion. She had done everything she could, knowing Tanya would not come in to sniff the fragrance of Naomi's cleaning detergent and nod her head in approval as always. The special feeling of satisfying Tanya was missing.

Naomi adjusted her cleaning apron as she stepped toward the house. She held her cleaning bag tightly as she walked with quick steps through Tanya's front yard. She could tell from the slightly ajar front door that Tanya was at home. She could imagine Tanya pulling her into a brief hug when they saw each other. Naomi knew that they could have been good friends if she didn't keep drawing back from Tanya. It always felt like Tanya wanted them to have something more than a house cleaning contract, but Naomi wasn't keen on getting too close because she didn't trust her feelings around Tanya. She had been investing her time outside her cleaning in Seth, but he had turned out to be a giant asshole. It was true that they were only friends, but it had looked as if they were working on something more. They had even shared a kiss two days before she caught him out on a date with another girl. It was sickening as she thought about the situation now. She surely deserved better than that narcissist.

Naomi knocked lightly on the door. She decided to enter when she didn't hear anything unusual, so she would let herself inside. She knew that Tanya must be somewhere in the house, but she might not have heard her first knock.

The door emitted a gentle creak as Naomi stepped into the house. The living room was empty as she had imagined. The TV was on a channel where two identical-looking guys were singing a duet on a stage in front of three judges. She unzipped her bag and began to take out her supplies. She stopped short when she heard the sound of footsteps from the bedroom. Almost instantly, she saw Tanya and a tall, dark-haired girl step into the living room. Tanya's blond hair was ruffled, and her neck and face glistened with sweat. She tapped the girl's round ass, and they both giggled.

"Oh! Hello, Naomi," Tanya said when she noticed her for the first time.

Naomi could not put the finger on why she felt jealous when Tanya touched the young girl's ass. It was the same sense of betrayal that she had felt when she thought about Seth being a player and lying to her, although this felt... worse.

What's wrong with you? You don't have any right to feel jealous, Naomi's internal voice snapped.

"Naomi?" Tanya called again when she didn't get a response the first time.

"Hi," Naomi tried to force her face into a smile, but she didn't quite succeed. "I'm happy you are back. Is she fine now, your mom, I mean?"

"Yeah, she is. Thanks for asking," Tanya said before she turned to face the dark-haired beauty beside her. No words were exchanged, but Naomi caught Tanya winking at the other girl. In a blink, the girl walked out of the house, but not before she sent an intense gaze in Naomi's direction. There was an unspoken enmity between them. Naomi could tell that she had somehow concluded that Tanya had eyes for her, and she didn't look pleased.

When Naomi looked away from the other girl, she found Tanya staring at her with eyes that gave away her desire.

Had Tanya not just had sex with this other girl? Why was she looking at her that way? Naomi looked away from her employer with a twisted smile on her face and concentrated on the cleaning.

"Damn, I need a shower," Tanya said as she began to turn away from the living room, then she stopped suddenly and added, "You wanna join me?"

Naomi's throat went dry at that point. The flirty look on Tanya's face suggested that she really wanted Naomi in that shower with her. She was tempted to say yes, to finally give in to the sensual urges that she had always felt around Tanya. To experience the taste of Tanya's lips and the feeling of her boobs against hers.

Tanya noticed Naomi's hesitation, and she laughed. For a moment, Naomi thought she was going to come close and do something to hasten her decision, but Tanya only turned away and walked out of the living room, apparently to take that shower alone. Naomi heaved a sigh when Tanya left. If she had asked the question a second time, she would likely have given in. She had been running away from the attraction she felt for Tanya for too long because she didn't understand it. There had never been a time in her life when she thought she was into women, but Tanya had changed everything for her...

But she was fucking that dark-haired girl. She's clearly a player too! Focus on your damn cleaning, Naomi thought. As much as it looked like the girl was a one-night stand that Tanya had picked up to satisfy her guilty pleasures, it still mattered to Naomi that Tanya had done that. It was not different from what Seth had done, and if she had to be honest with herself, seeing Tanya with someone else had hurt a lot more.

"This is so messed up," Naomi said under her breath. She decided to just focus on the reason she was in Tanya's house.

The image of Tanya standing alone under the shower floated into Naomi's head as she ran her hands down her vacuum. She imagined herself in the bathroom with Naomi, kissing and rubbing their wet bodies against each other. Naomi felt her nipples pushing against her bra as these thoughts ran through her head. She found it remarkable that she was turned on by the idea of kissing Tanya when an actual kissing session with Seth had not produced that kind of reaction from her body. Was that the big sign that she was into women? She knew the truth —it was only difficult for her to embrace. The only answer was to keep on cleaning until she scrubbed the thoughts away.

A FEW DAYS later

Tanya's mind was a bag of mixed emotions. She had felt a massive buildup of her attraction to Naomi since she returned from her visit to see her mother. She had seen Aliana and her partner when her mom was in the hospital, and now she felt the need for companionship even more. Once her mother had stabilized, Tanya made her way home and tried to reach out to Peggy, an old fling of hers. She thought maybe that would take her confusing thoughts away from Naomi.

With no success contacting Peggy, she had tried the Rainbow Bar next, and it was there that she had seen Candy, the dark-haired girl she had brought home the last time Naomi came to clean. Tanya smiled now as she remembered the animosity that she had observed between the two. She had been even more surprised by the hurt expression that had crept onto Naomi's face. She had tried not to read too much meaning into that look, but it was hard not to wonder if Naomi was into her in that way. Her thoughts collided as Naomi was currently in the house, cleaning away. *Just keep it professional, you always speak before you think with women.* Tanya gazed at Naomi, who was across the room, working hard to deep clean.

Everything about her appealed to Tanya, from her

pretty face and curvy body to her hard-working dedica-
tion. She was struggling to keep her eyes away from her.
Naomi had left without a word the day Tanya brought
Candy home. Could it be that she was that hurt, and the
only way she could register her displeasure was to slink
away without waiting for the usual talk that they had
when she was done with her work? Tanya wasn't sure
about anything. Naomi was a complicated person. One
moment, you would think she was on the same page with
you, and in the next, she would give the impression that
she didn't know what you were doing.

"I should just focus on the TV," Tanya muttered under
her breath.

"Sorry, come again?"

"No, not you," Tanya said.

"Okay," Naomi said, returning her attention to the
table she was dusting.

Tanya tried to distract herself from staring at Naomi
by fixing her eyes on the television, but she didn't find
much entertainment in watching the music videos
showing on the screen. Her eyes flicked back over, and it
happened that Naomi had been looking at her too. It felt
like a high school romance movie where the girl was
crushing on the silent boy in the class, but he didn't seem
interested.

"I'm done," Naomi said as she stepped forward with
her bag. Tiredness was boldly written on her face, but she
looked like she would stick around for a chat today if
Tanya still felt like talking.

"That's great," Tanya said. "And you are not going to
make it later this week?"

"Yeah, I want to attend my brother's coding competition, you know, to cheer him on. I'm the only sibling he has," she said to Tanya.

Tanya felt like that was the most she had learned about her employee since she took her on to clean her house. Naomi wasn't exactly forthcoming with information about herself. She talked less, preferred to listen, and usually didn't have much to say when Tanya forced her to say something.

"That's nice," Tanya remarked. A week was a long time not to see Naomi in her house. With this twice-a-week schedule, Naomi had become a solid part of her routine. She didn't say much, and she quickly retreated when things were getting too hot for her, but she was the only companionship that Tanya could point to in her life right then. She was more than a cleaner to Tanya, so much more, but it had just started to become apparent when faced with the thought of losing her.

"Before you go," Tanya began, and she stopped for a moment to observe Naomi's face. She saw sheer curiosity in it. "I want you to know that the offer to join me in the shower still stands."

Naomi's face flushed slightly, and she swallowed the way she had done when Tanya made the shower suggestion the first time. That hesitation was back again. Naomi wanted it, but something was holding her back.

Tanya took a step forward and wrapped an arm around Naomi's neck, pulling her in for a kiss. The way Naomi's eyes squeezed shut told Tanya that she had been thinking of this moment for a long time. The moment their lips touched, Tanya knew that she wanted to kiss those lips forever. They were soft against hers, yielding to the gentle probing of her tongue.

We are kissing. We are fucking kissing, Tanya screamed in her head as she explored the edges of Naomi's passion. They were holding each other tight while their tongues danced to the rhythm of their desire for each other. Tanya had imagined this moment many times before, but nothing she dreamed came close to the reality of holding Naomi while she was still dressed in her cleaning apron. Tanya had fun with many women over the years, but that's all it was—just fun. Sometimes it was just a way to allow her to feel something.

Feeling the need to turn the heat up a little bit more, Tanya took her right arm off Naomi's neck and reached out to touch her breasts. All the built-up magic of that moment instantly dissipated as Naomi drew back from Tanya like someone who had been stung by something venomous. Tanya tried to salvage the sweet experience by attempting to pull Naomi back into the kiss, but the girl took a step back, giving the impression that she was no longer interested in what they had both enjoyed a few moments ago.

Tanya saw the confused look on Naomi's face and realized that the girl had yet to truly understand her sexuality.

"I... I need to go now," Naomi said. Beads of sweat had popped up on her forehead.

You are not a fucking sixteen-year-old who has to keep running away when something threatens your perceived choice of sexuality! Yet Tanya only smiled and told Naomi it was fine.

"I'm sorry for touching you that way," Tanya said. She knew that Naomi would have been satisfied to continue kissing her for longer. Caressing her had ruined everything. Tanya had no regrets, though. It was enough that she had tasted Naomi's lips, for now.

"Yeah, it's fine," Naomi mumbled and quickly walked

to the door. Her bag jiggled as she rushed out of the house. Tanya watched her leave with a tinge of disappointment that everything had happened so fast and ended so abruptly. She was fairly sure that this would not be the last time she would kiss Naomi. Tanya knew the girl would come back to her when she had allowed herself to be who she was. *Or she might never come back?*

Naomi had looked really disturbed when Tanya had touched her breast. There was the possibility that she could chalk Tanya off her client list and never set foot in her house again. You fucking fool, Tanya thought to herself as she looked down at the floor before burying her face in her hands. She had to wait a week to learn Naomi's decision. She could call before then, but she thought it would be super creepy to disturb her with calls after what has just happened. She decided to wait and see what Naomi was going to do. The girl had enjoyed the kiss, no doubt. Why had she stopped when Tanya tried to push things a little further? Tanya wondered if she had somehow triggered a bad memory for Naomi when she had touched her. All of these thoughts were spinning around Tanya's mind. This didn't usually happen to her as she was not an over-thinker, but something about Naomi had changed that.

Tanya switched the channel away from music, hoping to catch an interesting film on the movie channel. She sighed as she sunk down into the couch and attempted to figure out the impact this woman was having on her mind.

6

N aomi didn't drive home after she left Tanya's house. She had driven her car around the nearby streets, trying to clear her head after everything that happened. She had seen the kiss coming for some time, but it had felt so unreal when it happened —so out of the world that she had been scared by it. None of the men she had kissed had ever felt like that before. The way Tanya kissed her and touched her had been nothing short of amazing.

But I ruined it!

Naomi clenched a fist and felt the urge to slam it against the wheel in front of her. She had pulled back when she felt Tanya's hand on her boobs because it reminded her of the silent dark-haired girl that she had seen with Tanya the last time around. The moment she remembered that girl, it had been easy for her to pull herself out of Tanya's embrace. She had really felt those kisses, and she was getting more confirmation about her sexual leanings with the overly positive way her body had responded to the kiss. But she wasn't sure Tanya was the right woman for her. Her anxiety told her that Tanya would just lead to tears.

She had driven her car around for over an hour, and it was getting dark already. She knew that she had to return home. With the events at Tanya's still swirling in her head, Naomi was not sure what she should do next. She knew that the next time she was in Tanya's house, they would likely go farther than where they had gone today.

She thought about the situation again and realized that she could not accuse Tanya of leading her into something she was unwilling to do. All along, she had been conscious of the growing tension between them. Tanya wasn't trying to force her sexuality on her. Instead, she was helping Naomi learn and embrace the truths about herself that she had been trying her hardest to ignore.

"Still haven't embraced it yet," Naomi grumbled as she turned the wheel of the car, making a turn that would take her back to the street where her home was. She thought it was amusing that she and Tanya both stayed alone and needed friendship outside the businesses they ran. It made sense that Tanya was feeling lonely, too, and they just found companionship in each other. But Naomi felt terrified about taking that next step.

Is it about commitment now, or are you scared of who you really are?

Naomi kept her eyes on her house, knowing that she needed to get inside and process her thoughts. She pushed thoughts of Tanya Smithson aside and began to think about Jerry's competition. In a few moments, Naomi pulled into her driveway. She got out of the car, not forgetting the bag that held her cleaning supplies. She had her cleaning apron on and couldn't wait to take it off and go wash her body off in the bathroom.

She went inside the house and flopped down on a chair first. Thoughts of Tanya threatened to come back, but she managed to keep them at bay. She thought, instead, of what to do for the rest of the evening, but no ideas really appealed to her. Rather, it was the mental image of her lips locked in a passionate kiss with Tanya's that played in a never-ending loop in her mind. Naomi felt the strong urge to pull down her pants and slip her fingers deep inside her underwear to finish the feeling of pleasure that had begun at Tanya's. She decided not to resist the urge, knowing that she needed a release. With a tiny moan, Naomi undid the zipper of her pants and took everything off to explore her wetness.

THE FOLLOWING DAY, Tanya sat on the edge of her bed, trying to sort out her feelings. She missed Naomi badly, but she had not called to find out what the problem was in fear of pushing her further away. Naomi had gone to give her brother moral support for a competition, and Tanya thought it best not to meddle in her affairs now that she was away from her. *Maybe time apart was a good thing, right?*

She sighed as she remembered her failed attempt last night to get Naomi out of her head with a visit to the Rainbow Bar to pick another girl. Rainbow Bar, I just cannot get used to that damn name, she thought. She went to the club, looking for someone with similar features to Naomi, and she succeeded. She and the girl spent some time drinking at the bar before Tanya drove them to her house. They had jumped at each other the moment they got inside the house. They ran their hands over each other's bodies, and they kissed passionately. But it wasn't anything like the short but earth-shattering kiss with Naomi.

Sex with "Rainbow Bar" girl wasn't bad, but it wasn't great either, and Tanya knew it was her fault. She wasn't tuned in completely to what they were doing. She was still thinking of Naomi as her recent pickup teased her wetness, which was solely due to thoughts of Naomi. What could have been a terrific fuck was marred by the fact that she was distracted. The girl had picked up her jacket and left the same night, and she was long gone before Tanya remembered that she had not even asked her name.

Tanya stood up and paced around the room. She had hoped the girl she brought home would stay over, just to fill the quiet void in her home. Just to help her forget. *You're losing your cool, and you have to focus on work and making money. Women only get in the way,* Tanya thought to herself as if her internal parent role was taking over.

Maybe a Naomi look-alike wasn't a good idea. She would have been better off with someone completely different, someone whose face would not remind her of Naomi at every turn. Next time, she would not make the same mistake.

She looked out the window and saw that it was early dawn. It was an hour or two earlier than her usual wake-up time. She would have loved to get back in bed and get some proper sleep, ahead of the workload she had for the day. It was clear that it was going to be tough falling back asleep after everything she had thought about in the time that she had been awake. These thoughts would float in her head and would keep her wired.

Her eyes glanced toward her phone as she felt an urge to call Naomi, but she stopped herself and threw her mobile in the bedside drawer. She didn't want to get in her way. If Naomi really wanted to be there, she would be. Tanya knew she shouldn't try and influence her decisions. Sexuality could be a pretty confusing concept.

After splashing some cold water over her tired eyes in the bathroom, Tanya sat back down on the bed. Remembering that she wanted to chat with her sister to find out how their mother was faring at the moment, Tanya reached for her phone in the drawer. She saw that Aliana was not online, so she sent her a text. She checked Aliana's avatar and saw the picture of her partner and their adopted kids, all smiling.

"I deserve to be happy too,' Tanya muttered as she turned off the display on her phone. She remained sitting in the darkened room, thinking about how her happiness was linked to Naomi Lawson. Maybe the moment would pass, and she would find someone who she liked more than Naomi. Someone who was already gay and would not need to be guided through the process of acknowledging her sexual preferences. If Naomi didn't want to be hers, it would be tough, but Tanya would move on. It wasn't the first time she had suffered such heartbreak.

7

Tanya swept Naomi into a big hug. It was the first time they had seen each other since Naomi left to attend her brother's competition in a nearby town. Naomi had come around, not to clean, but to say hello to her employer. Tanya hugged her even tighter when Naomi revealed that her kid brother was one of the finalists in the competition.

"I missed you," Tanya whispered to Naomi when they pulled away from each other.

Naomi drew in a sharp breath before she replied in the same manner, "Missed you, too, Tanya."

Words were no longer needed from that point forward. Naomi could see the unbridled passion in Tanya's eyes, mirroring the same thing she felt. She had decided to accept the part of her that loved Tanya. Why did she have to keep searching for male company when there was someone she admired so much? Naomi knew she had to embrace her true self.

Naomi and Tanya wrapped their arms around each

other for the second time that evening and began to kiss with all the desire they felt. Naomi thought their first kiss had been slow and sensual, but this one was all about their pent-up desires. Naomi shuddered as Tanya's hand slid up her top until it landed on her breast. This time, no one pulled back. She knew that she wanted this, and there was no going back now that they had started. They continued to kiss passionately, exploring every corner of each other's bodies with their hands. Tanya pulled back from Naomi's kiss at one point, causing the latter to wonder what was going on.

"Let's go to my room," Tanya whispered.

Naomi nodded her head in agreement, and she let Tanya lead the way towards the bedroom. *The same bedroom where she fucked the dark-haired girl.* Naomi decided it didn't matter anymore. The time away given her time to think—a lot.

She knew what Tanya felt for Naomi wasn't the same as what she had felt for the other girl. There was some special connection between her and Tanya, and she had always known it. It was only now that she was finally letting it happen.

Naomi had been in Tanya's room before to clean the floor, dust the window sills, and other things related to her work, but today, she was there in a different capacity. She and Tanya resumed kissing the moment they stepped into the room. Naomi could feel Tanya's soft body through the fabric of her silk gown. They kissed, touched each other, and kissed some more. Naomi felt weak in the knees as Tanya flicked her tongue around her earlobe. She held on to Tanya's body for support because it felt like she was going to fall.

"We can take it as slow as you want to," Tanya muttered.

"Trust me, I've been fantasizing about you since the moment we met. I want you so badly, Tanya. I've been terrified to be honest with myself, and I don't know why," Naomi replied.

Tanya helped Naomi out of her shirt and the denim pants that she wore. In just a matter of a few moments, they were both down to their underwear, desperately eager to cover each other's bodies with kisses and touches. Naomi felt a rush of pleasure as Tanya drew tiny circles on her nipples with her fingers, making her breasts ache for more. She bit her lips as Tanya circled her hands around her back to unhook her bra.

"Goodness," Naomi breathed when she felt the touch of Tanya's lips against her bare nipples. It was so sudden and so pleasurable. The warmth of Tanya's tongue on her sensitive tips made her toes curl. She looked at Tanya, and the expression on her face suggested that she was just getting started and had more coming for Naomi.

"I've been desperate for you," Tanya moaned.

Naomi tried to take off Tanya's bra, too, but Tanya wasn't ready for her to do that yet. Tanya nudged Naomi onto the bed, and she laid there, her chest rising and falling slowly as she took each breath. Tanya closed the gap between them as she set her mouth against Naomi's thighs, gently kissing her way up toward Naomi's wet core.

Naomi let out quiet moans as she experienced wave after wave of pleasure from Tanya's kisses. Her moans grew louder as Tanya's lips drew closer to her clit. She fisted the silky sheets tightly when Tanya pulled her panties aside and flicked her clit with her tongue. She could not understand why this felt more pleasurable than any previous experiences she had with the guys she had dated in the past. *It must be true. I'm so fucking gay.*

Tanya removed Naomi's underwear, leaving her completely naked. Naomi's moan was louder than ever when Tanya kissed her inner thighs while circling her clit with her finger. She could feel her clit swelling, straining against every moment of Tanya's touch. Her eyes rolled back in their sockets from the overwhelming amount of pleasure she felt with everything Tanya did to her. She was stroking the top of Naomi's vagina with her tongue now, strokes that forced Naomi's toes to curl. Naomi squeezed her breasts in response to Tanya's touches. Never had any of Naomi's previous sexual partners paid so much attention to her needs. The goal with those guys was usually to get her wet, and then they would penetrate her before thrusting away—entirely forgetting about her needs after that point. Tanya was completely different. She knew the right spots to touch to whip Naomi's body into a frenzy.

Tanya moved her warm tongue in long strokes from Naomi's clit down to her wet opening. Naomi could feel something building up in her, and she knew that if Tanya didn't stop what she was doing, she would experience an orgasm for the first time without having to do it herself. She had hit the "Big O" many times before during intense sessions of rubbing her clit and squeezing her tits late in the night, but she had never reached orgasm with any of the guys she had fucked before. It was a one-way game with them.

Naomi marveled at how Tanya took things slowly, paying attention to every part of her body. She had kissed her everywhere—from her toes to her knees to her erect clitoris—and every place Tanya's lips touched had left a trail of fire that made Naomi writhe with pleasure.

She made another attempt to reach for Tanya's bra to take it off, but Tanya evaded her hands and continued to give her pleasure with the experienced movements of her mouth and fingers. Naomi was on the edge of her eventual release, but Tanya did not stop pushing her even further into bliss. Tanya took a moment to take off her underwear, and she rejoined Naomi on the bed. Tanya spread Naomi's legs wider, so she could mount her with ease. Tanya set her clit against Naomi's and began to move her groin back and forth so that their clits rubbed together.

Naomi had never imagined that anything could feel so good. She wrapped her hands around Tanya's ass, increasing the speed they moved against each other.

"You like this?" Tanya asked her as they kept grinding against each other.

"Yeah, it feels great," Naomi moaned.

"There is something that feels even better," Tanya whispered, and Naomi wondered what she had in mind.

They continued to rub themselves against each other as they both became wetter by the minute. Tanya was moaning this time while Naomi felt she would have cum by now if Tanya had not stopped giving her head. Tanya rolled off her after a few more minutes, and she collapsed on the bed, panting. It was clear that she had enjoyed herself. Was this the end? Naomi asked in her head. Tanya had started so well, but in the end, Naomi had been left high and dry in the same way the guys she had been with usually did. Sex was over the moment they shot their jizz wherever they pleased.

It took a few seconds before Tanya got off the bed and reached for something Naomi could not see in the room's dim lighting. The hum that filled the room at that moment told Naomi what Tanya was up to.

"Let's hear you moan, baby," Tanya said as she turned back to face Naomi.

She urged Naomi's legs apart and gently set the silicone vibrating shaft against her clit. Naomi's eyes widened as she felt the impact of the vibrator. The feeling was divine, unable to think of any other way to describe it.

"Hold it," Tanya said, offering Naomi the vibrator.

Naomi's hands were too shaky to hold the vibrator properly at first, but she was able to get a good grip after a few tries. Now that she was in control of the vibration, she moved it up and down the length of her slit and around her clit. With moans continuously pouring from her open mouth, Naomi saw Tanya looking at her with a smile on her face.

"Alright, let's take this one step further. I have so much that I want to do to you," Tanya said suddenly. She turned away from Naomi again, rummaging through a drawer.

Naomi was focused on the exquisite pleasure that was shooting throughout her body. The orgasm that had slipped away from her earlier was building up again, and now that she was in control of the vibration, she would let it buzz until she reached the peak of sexual satisfaction. Her eyes struggled to remain open as she edged toward climax with each passing moment.

She felt the touch of a hard object against her wet entrance, and she opened her eyes wide to see what Tanya was up to. She saw Tanya holding a thick metal dildo. The coolness of the shaft was such a contrast to the heat of her pulsating core.

"Tanya... Ooh!" Naomi writhed as Tanya started to push in the hard metal, taking her breath away. As it probed deeper, Naomi tensed with pleasure as it reached her sweet spot. Naomi could not keep her moans quiet at this point. She was writhing on the bed as she felt an intense buildup of pleasure. Nothing was going to stop her from reaching orgasm this time.

Tanya took the clit stimulation out of Naomi's hands and used her mouth to suck on her clit hard as she drove the metal dildo inside of Naomi, deep and slow. After a series of thrusts that hit the right spots, Naomi's face flushed, and she felt a shiver spread over her body, followed by an intense urge to pee.

"Don't hold it back," Tanya urged her. It sounded like Tanya's voice was far away.

Naomi unclenched the muscles of her vagina, and a stream of clear, odorless liquid gushed out of her.

"Fuck, this is so hot," Tanya chuckled as she slowed down the movement of the dildo as Naomi's orgasm continued to pulsate over her clit and throughout her body.

Naomi was still panting, unable to fully understand these new sensations. She hadn't cum like that since... well, never.

"Fuck, I haven't ever squirted before. I didn't know I could. Have you?" Naomi asked as she sat up slightly, with her head tingling as she spoke. She supposed that was another effect of cumming so hard.

"Yeah, if you can touch the right spots," Tanya said with a smile across her face.

It was Naomi's turn to push Tanya on the bed. "Let's hear you moan now."

Naomi took off Tanya's bra and tossed it aside. She then put her head between Tanya's legs and lapped up the wetness that was beginning to trickle down the inside of her thigh. It was clear that Tanya had enjoyed fucking Naomi just as much as she hoped. Tanya grabbed Naomi's head, taking control of the oral simulation. She ground her hot core into Naomi's mouth, which led her to cum intensely. Tanya moaned as her eyes rolled back, enjoying every single moment.

8

Naomi had just returned from a meeting with a prospective client, and she was tired, mentally and physically. The woman had spoken as if she was a big bundle of trouble, and Naomi wasn't sure she wanted to work for someone like that. She had enough clients on her hands, enough to make her consider employing someone else to work with her. She was pleased to have new customers, but the first impression she had of that woman was terrible.

She stepped out of her car with her bag and headed toward her house. She thought of curling up on her couch to watch TV while she ate dinner. That was the best way she could think of to cool off for the evening after the stressful day she just had.

Naomi had barely entered the house when her phone began to ring. She dropped her bag on the floor and pulled her phone out of her pocket. The name on her screen was that of someone she had not seen in three years. It was her ex-boyfriend, Jack, and to be fair, her memories of their time together were mostly positive. She had left him because she wanted to concentrate on her cleaning business, and he could be a little boring sometimes. It took a while before she swiped the call button and listened to the voice on the other end of the call.

"Hello," Naomi said.

"Hi, Naomi," Jack said. His voice was deep and assured as it had always been since she met him. "It's great to hear your voice. How are you?"

Naomi waited a few seconds before replying to Jack. She was still wondering why Jack had called her. She thought he would have long since forgotten about her.

"I'm fine, Jack," she replied. "I'm surprised you called."

"I haven't forgotten about us," Jack said. "I've been away traveling, and I've done a lot of thinking. The time we spent together was everything. The memories are stuck in my head. I want us back together as we were before."

Naomi was not sure how to react to what Jack had just said to her. She thought she had ruined the relationship that she had with him forever when she had put her foot down and insisted that she wanted out. He was such a kind and sweet guy.

"Are you there?"

"Yeah," Naomi said. "I don't know. It's been so long."

"Your business is settled now, isn't it? Look, I have to be honest with you. I've been doing a lot of meditation and thinking about what matters to me."

"Yeah, business is great. Umm, about the other..."

"Are you going out with someone else then?" Jack asked after Naomi hesitated.

Naomi was on the verge of saying yes, and then she thought about Tanya. They definitely had something going on. It was true that they had not officially started anything *serious*, but the mind-blowing sex was something exceptional. She wasn't going to forget it for a long time. It felt as if her whole life had changed after that sexual encounter with Tanya, yet she still felt drawn to Jack's offer. She felt drawn towards the familiar comfort of heterosexuality, seeing how it was what she was used to.

"Are you there?"

"Umm, sorry, I'm not in a relationship yet, but..."

"That's all I want to hear," Jack said. "I will be free tomorrow. Can we hang out sometime in the evening? Come on, let's just meet face to face. I really want to see you."

"Alright," Naomi said, "I'm free, so why not!"

Jack ended the call, and Naomi began to consider her situation. Now that Jack was back on the scene, Naomi began to doubt herself. She was already looking forward to seeing him and thinking of how they would reconnect with each other after a long time apart. They had gone through a lot together. Naomi dropped her phone back in her pocket and walked into the room to change her clothes. *Jack, Tanya... what a mess. At least Seth the dickhead was long gone.*

After three years, the excitement of seeing Jack started to push away her guilt about Tanya, who also played it so cool. Tanya gave off the impression she just wanted to have fun with as many women as possible. *What if I'm not even really gay? Maybe it was just a one-time thing? I can't imagine Tanya settling down with anyone.*

Naomi tried to shake off her whirling thoughts. Jack had been loyal when they were together, and if he was the same person she had dated until three years ago, she was going to be fine with him. He was what she knew of happiness. He was secure and safe.

Naomi took off her shirt and pants, slipping into a sleep shirt. She took a look at herself in the mirror—her eyes looked exhausted, with dark bags forming underneath them. Her hair was in order, and her face was in good shape, though. She smiled at her reflection in the mirror, revealing her sparkling white teeth. After a quick check of her reflection, Naomi made her way to the living and saw her workbag on the floor where she had dropped it to answer Jack's call. She picked it up and walked to the corner of the house that she reserved for her business stuff and then dropped the bag there. There, everything was neat and tidy. Everything had a place. Naomi didn't like things messy.

She walked back to the living room and sank her ass down onto the couch which was directly opposite the TV. She could not remember the last time she had sat down to watch TV in her house and became a total couch potato. She was always tied up with something or the other. Now, she sat on the couch with her eyes focused on the TV while she thought of what she could make for dinner. After brainstorming on what she could whip up from her nearly bare fridge, she decided to go for something she could put together quickly.

"Fried spaghetti it is," she muttered.

She continued watching TV for a while, enjoying the baseball game that was being played. She thought of Seth reaching a professional level like this, appearing on people's TV screens. It was still disappointing how he had blown the promising friendship that they could have had by sleeping around with anyone he could find.

It's just like you are about to do by ruining your friendship with Tanya.

Naomi let out a deep sigh as she thought about the

situation again. She had genuinely felt that special connection with Tanya, but Jack's call had changed the game. She thought Jack deserved a chance because she had left him for so long, and he still hadn't moved on. She could still back out of her relationship with Tanya since they had not yet gotten too deep.

Naomi stood up, her mind plagued with questions about her decision to sideline Tanya doe another opportunity with Jack. She decided to pick up the last packet of pasta from the fridge and set about cooking dinner. Her belly had begun to grumble, along with the confusion in her mind.

"It's all so confusing," Naomi mumbled.

∼

LATER THAT WEEK

Naomi was packing her stuff away when Tanya returned from work. Her mood always brightened whenever she was around Naomi. Tanya knew she had feelings toward Naomi, but she had no idea how to voice them. Business and sex were her strengths, with emotive communication as a weakness. They had not seen one another or had sex since, but the memories of that first encounter they had were stuck in her head. Tanya wasn't new to having sex with women, but the way Naomi had slid so comfortably into it surprised her. It reminded Tanya of a past lover named Selena, who also thought she was straight until she met Tanya.

"Hey. Naomi," Tanya said as she dropped her handbag on the table. Naomi looked up from the bag that she was filling with her supplies.

"Uh... hello," she replied. Tanya could tell by her tone that something was wrong.

"You okay?"

"Yeah, sure."

"Okay," Tanya said as she walked closer to the spot where Naomi had just gotten to her feet. Her bag was hanging loosely on her shoulder.

Tanya wrapped her hands around Naomi in a hug, not minding the cleaning apron that the younger woman had on. She noticed, however, that Naomi was stiff in her arms. Next, Tanya tried to place a kiss on Naomi's lips, but she moved her lips away slightly. It was definitely clear now that something was wrong.

"You want to talk to me about this or what? Is running hot and cold your forte?"

"There's nothing to talk about," Naomi said. Her voice was silent, cold.

"Is this about Jerry or your dad? What's going on, love?"

"My family is fine," Naomi said and wriggled herself out of Tanya's loose hug.

Tanya could not resist the urge to shake her head and roll her eyes. There were times when Naomi gave the impression that she was a high school girl involved in some romantic drama with her classmate. It was annoying when she decided to act this immaturely.

"So, you don't want to talk? It's fine," Tanya shrugged. She knew that Naomi would come around as she always had, and whatever was bothering her would be fixed later. Tanya decided to change her clothes in her room and think of what to do for the rest of the evening. Asking Naomi to stay with her was out of the question. In her current moody state, Naomi would end up pissing Tanya off rather than enjoying her company.

"My ex-boyfriend is back," Naomi announced as Tanya began to walk toward her room.

"Oh, and is that a problem?"

"Well, we split three years ago, but he's come back for me. He wants to try again."

Tanya turned back to face Naomi. "If he wasn't good enough for you three years ago, why do you think he is a good option now?"

"I was the cause of the breakup. He wasn't at fault," Naomi said. "He has come back to win my love again, and I'm drawn to him. I'm just finding it hard to tell you. This has all been very confusing for me. I hope you understand?"

"Drawn to him more than you are with me? And do you think that I am a cold hard rock with no emotions?" Tanya snapped before taking a deep breath to add, "I understand what you mean. I'm sorry," Tanya said.

"You don't talk about feelings, Tanya. You don't seem to find it hard to occupy yourself with women. I don't want to be another one added to the list," Naomi said.

"Yeah, it's all good. You deserve happiness," Tanya said. "Was that why you were moody when I came in? Come on, life goes on. It was fun while it lasted, wasn't it?" Tanya felt hurt, but she still couldn't get the words out to express how hurt she was. She didn't want to be an experiment either.

Naomi was staring at her now, and Tanya suspected she was trying to determine if she was truly hurt by her declaration. Tanya chuckled and blew Naomi a kiss before she walked away from the living room, feeling a surge of jealousy inside of her.

A few minutes after Tanya entered her room and walked over to the window, she heard Naomi leave. She noticed an unfamiliar car waiting for her across the road. *Mm, I bet he can't make her cum as I did.* Tanya's bitter words were just a way of protecting herself. She watched Naomi and her ex drive away as she refused to let her emotions get in her way any longer. It didn't matter who Naomi was dating now since the point was that Tanya had missed out on her, and maybe it was for the best. She hadn't been as focused on her work since Naomi had entered her life.

"Quite sad," she muttered as she took off the jewelry on her wrist and threw it down on the table. She had hoped she could make something special with Naomi, but it had all ended so suddenly. Now, she could only wish Naomi happiness, and she knew she wouldn't be messing around with any more curious women.

Maybe I need some fun. I should call Peggy.

Tanya reached for her phone. There was some distance between them, but that didn't matter when it was just a bit of fun. Tanya imagined what it would be like to have Peggy in bed with her after months of being apart. It would be explosive. She would channel all the frustration of losing Naomi to some guy into that sexual encounter. She knew how Peggy liked it, and she knew what she would receive in return.

"Gotta call Peggy," Tanya said as she began to undress and hit the call button.

9

Naomi had a sweet smile on her face as she walked back to the car with Jack. They had enjoyed themselves, dining at a new expensive restaurant in town. They had talked about old times, and Naomi had wondered why she had ruined something that was so wonderful in the first place. She could have tried her best to juggle her work with the relationship she had with Jack. The more she thought about it, the more she realized that it didn't make much sense to have denied herself happiness, all because she wanted her business to thrive.

You were so selfish back then, Naomi had thought to herself countless times.

It didn't feel like she had much choice back then, though. She had been at a crossroads, and she had no other option than to focus all her attention on her business. Naomi had to do it all to make her business survive and thrive, and her approach had paid off in the end. It had less to do with Jack, to be fair. It was more of her trying to survive in a world where she didn't have parents to support her. Her mother had died when she was a child, and her father refused to lift a finger to help her because he was mad about her decision not to go to college.

Naomi shook the dark thoughts out of her head. This was not the time to brood over what she didn't have. She felt grateful that the man she once loved had returned to her years after she had pushed him away.

"Thank you," Naomi said with a smile on her face as Jack opened the passenger door for her to slip inside. He was everything she remembered him to be—and more. He looked even better physically, with a broader chest and bigger arms, proving that he had been a regular at the gym in the years they were apart. She found him almost as big as Seth but way more attractive.

Jack got in beside her shortly after that. He buckled his seatbelt while keeping his eyes on Naomi. "You enjoyed it there, right?"

"Yeah, I did," Naomi said. "Thank you."

It had been wonderful sitting across from him, staring into his eyes and remembering the early days of their relationship. She knew that she had messed things up by leaving him the first time. She was going to make it work between them this time around.

"Okay," Jack said before turning his focus to the road.

Naomi had been visiting loads of fun places with Jack since he came back into town. She was enjoying this new phase of her life. Her business was profitable, and she had a man to give her all the attention she wanted and needed. He put her on a pedestal and made her feel special, like the only woman who ever mattered to him.

Naomi thought it was a good thing she had made the

decision to leave things where they were with Tanya. She just could not give Naomi the kind of attention that Jack could provide. Tanya was all about her business, and she really didn't have the time to hang out with Naomi as much as she would have liked. Naomi could vouch for Jack's loyalty, but she couldn't say the same about Tanya. Even though there was something still unexplainable about how she felt, Naomi was too worried she would get hurt by Tanya.

Jack drove away from the parking lot of the restaurant, steering the vehicle in the direction of Naomi's house. The soft R&B song that Jack played on the radio put Naomi at ease. She swayed her head slowly to the rhythm of the music. For a long while, she looked out through the window, watching the buildings flashing by. If she stared too long without distraction, she couldn't help but wonder how Tanya was doing.

"Are you okay?" Jack asked her.

"Yeah, sure," Naomi said.

Maybe she would tell Jack sometime in the future, but she could not tell him now when she was still struggling to get Tanya out of her mind. She had decided to be with Jack, and she was going to stick with it, but forgetting Tanya was not going to happen overnight. *It was just a silly fling, right?* Naomi smiled at Jack and then continued to look out of the window.

Jack's car rolled to a stop outside Naomi's house. He knew where she lived because he had brought her home on more than one occasion since they got back together. Sometimes, he would follow her in, and they would just talk about different things. With Jack, there was always a lot to talk about. They had not yet been intimate since Jack had returned, but she was sure that it would not take long before they would end up in bed together. She could see the growing desire for her in his eyes. She wanted him, too, but it was not her nature to push for these things. They would allow the lust for each other's bodies to keep building up until it got to the point where it could not be leashed anymore. Naomi was a little hesitant about something, but she presumed it was just nerves.

They both got out of the car. Naomi took one look at Jack and saw him staring right back at her.

"My God, you are so beautiful," Jack whispered.

"Thank you," Naomi smiled as she wrung her hands together. From the look on Jack's face, it appeared that he might have reached the end of his control over his desire for her body. His eyes roamed over her as if he could not wait to get his hands on her—to claim her back from anyone who tried to possess her. Naomi could feel the air between them charging with sexual energy. She was not surprised when Jack hurried toward her and pulled her in for a kiss. The cold night wind swept against Naomi's body as she stood outside her little house, but she found warmth in Jack's soft lips and arms.

But why are you still thinking of her?

NAOMI STARED at Jack's sleeping body on the bed, watching as his chest rose with each deep breath that he took. She could not believe how unsatisfying Jack had been in bed. In no way did he measure up to Tanya. He was only concerned with seeking his own release, caring nothing about her pleasure. Back in the day, before Naomi met Tanya, she would have called this kind of sex uneventful. But since that incredible experience in Tanya's bed, she had realized that sex was not just about a man's pleasure. The joy of it was in giving and receiving pleasure. Tonight, she had gotten the barest amount of pleasure from having sex with Jack. How anticlimactic, she thought to herself as she sighed quietly.

She shook her head as she continued looking at him, sleeping away after banging his way to orgasm without much thought to how she felt. She tried to remember if sex with Jack had always been this bad or if it was the incredible time she had with Tanya that made everything else pale in comparison. It was even worse when he had fallen asleep almost immediately after he ejaculated into the pink condom that he had slipped onto his cock before they got started. Naomi had found herself thinking of Tanya even when Jack was thrusting away. She couldn't stop herself from thinking of her.

Maybe it's not fair comparing them. Naomi rolled away from Jack on the bed. Tanya was always going to know how to please a woman better than Jack, but Jack's performance did not cut it at all. She had tried to direct him to what felt good, but he didn't seem to be paying attention. It was an utterly forgettable experience.

Naomi walked away from the bedroom and headed to the bathroom to clean her sweaty body. After the mind-blowing session with Tanya, what she had done with Jack tonight was a terrible follow-up. She would have to talk to him about being selfless in bed for a change. Maybe he would never be great at pleasing her as Tanya was, but he could do a decent job if he wasn't so concerned about mindlessly thrusting into her body. Maybe Tanya has ruined me with her magic tongue and fingers, Naomi wondered as she giggled.

Naomi wasn't sure if she had been fooling herself by

following what felt comfortable. All she was sure of was
that everything was a comparison against Tanya's
generosity in bed, and every thought was tainted by her.
Every feeling was owned by her. Everything was creeping
back towards Tanya Smithson.

"I'm not a lesbian," Naomi muttered. She didn't sound
convincing as she stared at herself in the mirror. It felt
more like she was attracted to women, but she had been
forcing herself to ignore that part of her. She could not
deny that she was attracted to Tanya. If she had any questions about her sexuality, something that remained clear
was that Tanya was the only one who gave her some
clarity

Naomi untied her towel and stepped into the shower.
She turned on the tap and exhaled sharply as she felt the
jets of cold water pounding her skin. She imagined Tanya
standing under the shower with her, kissing her and
rubbing her tits against Naomi's erect nipples. Naomi
tried to shake off the thoughts of making out with Tanya,
but the mental images were too powerful to ignore.

With a sigh of resignation that she was on her own,
Naomi leaned against the wall, reached down to her opening, and touched herself. She caressed her boobs with one
hand and rubbed her clit with the fingers of the other
hand. She made slow circular motions, doing it the way
Tanya had done. Droplets of cool water from the shower
mixed with the moisture between Naomi's thighs as she
teased her clit and squeezed her breasts harder.

Tanya is rubbing my clit, driving her finger into me,
she thought to herself as her eyes closed.

Naomi parted her wet opening, running her fingers
down both sides of her dripping slit as she prepared to slip

a finger inside. Her mind was fixed on Tanya. Everything she did to herself, she imagined it was Tanya who was touching and stroking her body. Her belly contracted, and her mouth flew open as she felt a tingle of pleasure run up her spine. She had inserted a second finger inside, making her body tremble. The speed of her strokes increased as she experienced a blissful build-up of pleasure. She was driving herself wild under the spray of the shower, writhing from the effect of her own touches. The sounds of her fingers plunging into her wet pussy filled the bathroom. She could feel her world shaking to its foundation as she kept moving her fingers in and out, fucking herself harder and faster.

Her fingers were pressing upward, as far as she could make them. Her vision blurred as she fucked her hot core, causing her body to shudder over and over again. She tried hard not to wake Jack up with her moans, but it was tough to keep her voice down with the way her body was reeling.

I want you so badly, Tanya.

Naomi's body spasmed as she climaxed—her fingers clenched by her tight, hot core. It was the height of pleasure for her. She collapsed against the wall as she lost the struggle to remain upright. Waves of sexual bliss washed over her, forcing her knees to buckle. Naomi nearly collapsed on the tile floor...

You need to sort this mess out, Naomi thought as she tried to steady her breathing. She remained in the shower with her back against the wall for some time. As she stood there, she thought about what being with Tanya again would feel like and how happy and excited she was to make it happen. As sweet as her time was with Jack, she felt no blazing passion like she did with Tanya. She thought about her mother dying young and how life was just far too short.

Naomi sighed and turned off the shower which exposed the loud snoring from Jack in the bedroom. She knew it would hurt his feelings, but better sooner than later.

10

Tanya had just sat through a meeting with Arte, the head of her company's promotion and publicity department. She had listened as he talked about the plans to push Marilyn's album forward. Marilyn was a new talent that the A&R team had brought in a few months back, and Tanya thought the singer was head and shoulders above any of their recent signings to the label. Arte had barely left Tanya's office when she got a text on her phone. For a moment, she thought it was business-related until she saw that it was from Naomi.

She straightened in her chair as soon as she saw that name. A new form of alertness came across her. She quickly went through the text.

We need to talk.

Tanya stared intently at the four words on her screen as if trying to discern a deeper meaning. She was happy that Naomi had reached out to her. Since that big guy came around, Naomi had withdrawn from Tanya in a way that she had not thought was possible. Even though Naomi was her cleaner first, Tanya realized that it wasn't just a fantasy. It was so much more. Naomi did something to her heart.

Things had been awkward, to say the least. Of course, the flirting stopped, but it reached the point where they couldn't even have a conversation without the tension growing. Tanya thought she would have to let her go. It always riled Tanya that *he*—she wouldn't allow herself to refer to him as Naomi's boyfriend—would pop up at her house to wait for Naomi to finish cleaning, eliminating any chance of Tanya and Naomi talking. Tanya knew they needed to have a healthy conversation to save their friendship, as it seemed that was all that was left.

Tanya sighed as she turned off her phone's screen. She wasn't going to feel too excited by Naomi's text because she knew that as long as Naomi was with that guy, things would not flow really well between them. And Tanya didn't have time for any more drama.

Maybe I should just turn straight.

Tanya quickly followed that thought with an abrupt head shake. She got out of her chair and walked toward the door of her office. Maybe when she got home, she could spare some time to call Naomi. Tanya was tired of Naomi's cold attitude and her boyfriend's—ugh, she hated that thought—policing nature. She waved to a few staff on her way out of the office complex. It had been a tiring day, and she looked forward to being back in her house to enjoy some time to herself.

Her phone began to buzz as she got near the parking lot. Without checking, she knew it was Naomi calling. She wondered at that moment if something was wrong. Was Naomi in danger or something? Tanya could not help feeling so protective.

"Hi, Naomi," Tanya said, keeping her voice level as she

spoke. She waved to Arte as he, too, got to the parking lot. "How are you?"

"I'm at your house. We need to talk," Naomi's gentle voice had a little steely edge to it.

All of Tanya's bitterness about losing her to that guy disappeared, and all she felt at that moment was concern. "Are you okay? Talk to me."

"Yeah, I'm fine. We'll talk when you get home."

By the time Naomi ended the call, Tanya was in her car, ready to drive as fast as she could to see Naomi. It was unclear what they were going to talk about, which troubled Tanya as she drove away from her office. She pressed down on the gas and got back home in record time.

Naomi was in the living room, seated on the couch when Tanya got in. She looked up as soon as Tanya entered the house and got to her feet. They stared at each other for what felt like an eternity, but it was probably just one long minute. Tanya took a step toward Naomi as she tried to understand what was going on in her head. She could not read anything from Naomi's face, and she found that a little bit strange.

"You are good, right? You're kinda freaking me out now!" Tanya said as she reached out with her hands and placed them on Naomi's shoulders.

Naomi replied with a nod while she kept her eyes fixed on Tanya. "I have done some serious soul searching…"

"Okay?" Tanya urged her to continue when it became clear that Naomi wasn't sure how to form her next words.

"Yeah, I have come to terms with the fact that I can't stop thinking about you, and maybe the fact that everything about you is better than anything else I have ever felt is because… well, because I think I might be gay. Or maybe I'm bisexual, or pansexual, or whatever. I just know I can't only be straight," Naomi said. "You know, it feels really great to finally say that out loud."

Tanya flung her arms open and hugged Naomi. Did this mean her clingy boyfriend was out of her life then? Now was not the time for questions, Tanya thought. What mattered was that Naomi had realized what made her happy, and Tanya hoped this time she wasn't going to run away from it.

"It's okay, sweetheart. You take all the time you need," Tanya squeezed her and gently kissed her forehead.

Two days later

Naomi got to Tanya's house earlier than usual as she wanted to get her cleaning jobs finished up early to surprise Tanya later that day. Her eyes squinted as the rays of the midday sun proved to be a little bit too harsh. She walked up to Tanya's door with her head brimming with thoughts of the euphoric sexual experience she had with Tanya the night they made up. Tanya had driven her to such heights of pleasure, and to her surprise, it went far beyond the last time. Jack didn't take the news well, but Naomi was putting herself first from now on.

She was about to get the spare key that Tanya had given her out of her bag when she saw that one of the windows was open. Naomi thought that it was not like Tanya to leave a window open when she wasn't around. Tanya was supposed to be at work, running the affairs of the record label. Naomi always had wondered what Tanya actually did at work since it seemed so elusive.

Naomi knocked on the door and waited for Tanya to

open up. She stared down at her nails while listening for sounds that might suggest Tanya was coming to open the door. Naomi knocked again as her mind flew back to the time she had walked in to see Tanya with that big-ass dark-haired girl. She hoped that things had changed. Nothing was exclusive, but Tanya clearly knew how Naomi felt about her.

She decided to attempt to open the door after two more knocks. Maybe Tanya was actually held up some-where in the house, or she was really at work, and she had only forgotten to close the window before leaving this morning. The door yielded when she turned the handle. Naomi stepped into the house, and her eyes quickly darted to the two cocktail glasses on the table. Naomi's heart began to beat faster. *Was this what she thought it was?*

"She probably just had a random guest visiting," Naomi muttered, but her reasoning didn't reassure her very much. It felt too similar to when she had walked in on Tanya and that other girl.

Naomi walked deeper to the living room. "Tanya?"

The TV was on, showing some crap daytime program. The sound was very loud, and Naomi guessed that was the reason Tanya had not heard her calling. Naomi was torn between turning down the TV volume and calling for Tanya again, but she soon decided that there was no use doing that. She had no business with the TV. She was here to clean the house, and she would do just that until Tanya showed up. *I'm sure it will all make sense soon, Naomi* thought.

She undid the zipper of her tool bag and began to get out her sprays. It was difficult to concentrate on getting ready to clean. Her eyes drifted to the two glasses on the table as she wondered what was going on. Where was

Tanya? Should she be worried that something had happened to her? Unable to bear the uncertainty of the situation, Naomi walked over to grab the TV remote and muted the loud music coming from the crappy program. Surely, if she called Tanya now, she would hear if she was in the house.

Naomi didn't need to shout Tanya's name again because as soon as she turned off the sound of the TV, she began to hear loud moans from Tanya's bedroom. No, it wasn't just Tanya giving herself pleasure. It sounded like some kind of sex party. Naomi fought back the urge to grab her bag and just walk out of Tanya's house. She gritted her teeth as she walked towards the bedroom, where the sounds were coming from. She wanted to see what was going on before reacting. She needed clarification once and for all.

You stupid girl, why did you trust her?

Her heart sank as she took each step toward the door. She could not believe that Tanya had jumped in bed with someone else just two days after she had made love with Naomi so passionately. Everything had seemed so perfect. Naomi got to the door and pushed it open. On Tanya's soft, bouncy bed, where Naomi had screamed until she was hoarse as Tanya set her body on fire just two days ago, Naomi saw two dark-haired women wearing nothing but thongs. They were kissing each of Tanya's boobs as she laid back on the bed, with her lips slightly parted and her eyes closed.

Tanya's eyes suddenly flew open, and Naomi found herself staring into those once calming blue eyes. Tanya was here having a fucking threesome. It was tough to wrap her head around what she was seeing. It was too much for her to bear.

"Don't call or text me ever again!" Naomi said and quickly turned away from the sickening sight in front of her.

Naomi thought it was bold of her to have believed that Tanya cared. She had obviously never cared. Naomi was nothing but a plaything to her—a girl Tanya could take advantage of because she was confused about her sexuality. There was nothing Tanya could say to convince her that she cared because her actions had proved otherwise.

"Shit! Naomi, wait!" Tanya called from the bedroom as Naomi hurried to the living room. She dropped the spare key on the side table and grabbed her work bag off the floor. She was done with Tanya forever. There was no going back.

11

T anya sat in her car and stared at the building with the bright, colorful neon lights outside. She had driven down to the Rainbow Bar to get thoughts of Naomi out of her head, but so far, she had not gotten out of her car. She sat there in the driver's seat, watching as people strolled in and out of the bar, sometimes in pairs. She could not give herself the mental push to get out of the car just yet because her mind was under siege by dozens of thoughts about Naomi Lawson. Tanya could not understand how she had become so emotionally dependent on Naomi. It was scary how much she had still been thinking about the girl now that they were no longer together. She had thought that burying herself in office work was going to take her mind off Naomi, but that plan did not just work.

I messed it all up with my stupid lack of self-control, Tanya thought as she continued to look at the people who were streaming into the bar. The dark, moonless sky mirrored her gloomy frame of mind. She had not yet gotten over the fact that Naomi did not want to see her ever again. She had stopped showing up for house cleaning duties, and she didn't answer or return any of Tanya's calls or texts.

Tanya wished she had turned down that WhatsApp message from Peggy, asking where she was because she wanted to meet. Tanya had been unable to reach Peggy since she had moved back into town, so she had been excited when she got that text from Peggy. The prospect of a threesome with Peggy had made her forget about Naomi's schedule. It had been the wrong decision to make, whether Naomi had walked in on them or not. She should not have done that when she knew she was building something meaningful with Naomi, and she could only hold herself responsible. Tanya could detach emotions from sex quite easily, especially when it came to her no-strings-attached, fun-only acquaintances such as Peggy.

Worst of all, the threesome wasn't even worth it. Peggy was more obsessed with her own needs and the other girl, and Tanya just had the house and an open-minded sexual nature.

"It's over," Tanya said with an air of regret. If she could go back to that moment when she answered Peggy's WhatsApp text, she would undoubtedly have worded her reply differently.

The decision to come to this bar was not an attempt to find someone who could fill the void left by Naomi because Tanya was not sure she could find someone who could connect with her that well. She and Naomi had gotten to know each other well, and she had learned about Naomi's geeky brother and strict father. There was more to their relationship than sex, and Tanya had enjoyed every bit of the time she had spent with Naomi.

Tanya snapped out of her musings when she heard a knock on the window of the car. She saw a friendly-looking guy with a blue Mohawk standing next to her window.

"Hey, you've been sitting here for a long time. I saw when you drove in, and I didn't see you get out of the car. I had to come and check if everything is okay," the dude said. Tanya saw from his outfit that he was one of the bouncers at the bar.

"Yeah, I'm fine," Tanya said. She instantly unhooked her seat belt and opened the door. She had already driven down to this place, so she decided to socialize and move on from the unfortunate situation with Naomi. She had lost the companionship that she had been looking forward to for so long, all because she could not resist getting a piece of Peggy's ass. She knew her self-destructive behavior was linked up with sex. That was an issue that delved way back, but she didn't want to dwell on that tonight.

Tanya stepped out of her car, inhaling the air that reeked of beer and cigarettes. She started walking towards the front door of the bar while doing her best not to think about Naomi anymore. They were done. There was no use mentally beating herself up over the mistake she made with her threesome with Peggy. She had burned their relationship, and there was no option but to move on.

She walked past another security guy on her way into the bar. She remembered the last time she had been here to look for a Naomi lookalike to keep her bed warm. It hadn't turned out well. Now, she was here again, but this time all she wanted was to have fun. She would have a drink or two in the company of people like her around whom she could feel safe. She would be careful not to get drunk because she had to drive back home. She would stay within her safe limit and just try to talk to people. She had to get Naomi out of her head and move on. Now that they weren't together anymore, Tanya wondered if Naomi would get involved with another woman any time soon. *Or maybe go back to her boyfriend.*

"Doesn't matter," she muttered as she strolled into the bar where people were having fun.

Tanya could see some girls at the bar, laughing as they downed shots of spirits. Some other girls were dancing to the music that filled the bar with thumping bass. Tanya walked past a group of guys who were listening to a girl say something that must have been really funny, judging by the way they were laughing. Tanya refused to strain her ears to listen to what the girl was talking about. She simply walked straight to the bar to order a vodka martini.

The bartender was still working on her cocktail when she felt a touch on her shoulder. Tanya turned and saw a pretty dark-haired lady smiling at her.

"Candy, hey, how are you?"

Candy took a seat beside Tanya. "I'm good. Haven't seen you since that day. You got pretty busy with work, yeah?"

"Yeah," Tanya said. "I didn't know you came here too."

"Why not?" Candy said, raising her dark brows. "Every lesbian comes here to be with their own people, even though the name is stupid. I mean, who thought of *Rainbow Bar*?"

"Yeah, so I heard," Tanya replied. The bartender placed the martini glass in front of her. "You care for a glass?"

"Nah. I don't drink. Not since pops had his kidney messed up."

"Oh, I'm sorry," Tanya said. "How is he now?"

"Dead," Candy said matter-of-factly. "It's been a long time. Ten years, I believe. I haven't tasted booze or anything since then."

"So, what do you do around here then?" Tanya said as she sipped her drink and savored the strong taste of alcohol in her mouth.

"It's about the people I see here," Candy said. "I just chill with people I know and sometimes meet new ones."

Tanya nodded as she took a few more sips from her glass. She had met Candy at a different bar, and they had got to talking, eventually agreeing to fuck each other based on pure attraction and desire for each other's bodies. They had not been in contact since then. It had been the perfect one-night stand.

"Yeah, I understand that," Tanya said as she set her glass back on the bar.

"So, how's that girl of yours that I saw with you that day?" Candy asked.

"You thought she was with me?"

"She looked mighty pissed when I came out with you, you know. I felt like I'd stepped on her property," Candy said. "Feelings. Deep feelings."

"Yeah, you are not wrong. We had something going for a while before I messed it up. She's over me already, and I have done the same."

Candy stared at Tanya for a long while as if she was trying to get into her mind and determine how she really felt about Naomi.

"I don't think so."

"What?" Tanya sputtered.

"You ain't over her."

"You are wrong."

"No, I'm not. I can see it in your face. That's why you are here. To get her out of your head, is that right?"

Tanya remained silent, knowing that Candy had figured her out too soon.

"Go and get her back. Apologize, buy her gifts, whatever. I can see you really like her. It's as clear as the moon out there. Okay, there's no moon tonight, but you get my point. Life is too short!" Candy encouraged Tanya.

"She's cut me off. I can't get through to her," Tanya argued before she drained her glass with a final gulp.

"Maybe you should just keep trying. You know what you want, and, hey, some people are worth chasing hard when you know how much they matter to you."

The rest of Candy's chatter flew right over Tanya's head. She couldn't stop thinking of trying again to get back with Naomi. It was true that she had been calling Naomi to no avail over the past few days, but there was another way she could tender her apology. She had thought of it before but had been reluctant to go that route. Now, motivated by Candy's words, she was ready to try again. She hoped she would be able to earn Naomi's forgiveness this time.

NAOMI WAS ON HER BED, staring at the number of missed calls that she had from Tanya. Whenever her phone buzzed with a call from Tanya, she would remind herself of how much she had hurt her and refuse to answer. She didn't want to hear Tanya's voice at all. It broke her heart to block her in such a way, but it was the only thing Naomi could do to protect herself from the toxic relationship between them. It was clear that the relationship was imbalanced, and Tanya wasn't as crazy about her as she had imagined.

She had thought of blocking Tanya's number, but she had kept herself from doing that—for now. Naomi had promised herself that if Tanya's calls became too much for her to handle, she would block her. She had hardened herself for this tough phase of their separation, knowing that she would come back stronger and would be able to find someone who valued her and loved her the way she deserved.

Naomi took her eyes off her phone screen and dropped the phone beside her. She looked forward to the days when she would have recovered entirely from this heartache over Tanya and when she would be free to spread her wings. *Maybe it was the age gap? Maybe that's why it hadn't worked out.*

"That's bullshit," Naomi whispered into the darkness. She had seen crazy age gaps in different relationships, and she knew that relationships failed not because of disparity in ages but usually because of breakdowns in love and trust.

I was dating myself.

As she laid back in the darkness, Naomi grudgingly conceded that she had probably expected too much from Tanya. Theirs was not a relationship that was based on commitment. Tanya had not asked Naomi to be her girlfriend or anything like that. Naomi knew that she could have done a better job establishing boundaries and talking about the relationship with Tanya. Instead, she had been carried away by the great sex, the joy of being that close to Tanya, and of embracing her sexuality.

"It's not gonna happen again," Naomi said to herself.

She was determined to not concede all the power in the relationship to her partner ever again.

She felt gloomy as she remained in her prone position on the bed. There were moments when tears flowed from her eyes at the thought of how Tanya had hurt her. She tried to keep from crying most of the time, but she could not help it when she felt overwhelmed by the thoughts of how amazing Tanya had been to her and how she had not suspected that she was having sex with other girls. She had built so much hope on her association with Tanya. It was sad how things had ended. Her first experience with a woman, completely shattered.

Naomi scrambled upright when she heard the knock on her door. She was not expecting anyone to come over this late. The knock came again, forcing Naomi to shout that she would be at the door in a moment. She adjusted her nightdress and hurried to the door. She wasn't sure who it was, but she would not put it past her neighbor, Samantha, who liked to get drunk at the nearby pub and knock on nearby doors afterward in hopes that she could start telling sad stories of her life.

Naomi was not in the mood to listen to Sam because she had enough with her own problems. She looked through the peephole and saw that it was not her neighbor, Sam, who was at the door. It was the most unlikely guest, given the current situation. It was Tanya Smithson. Her long blond hair was neatly pinned up, and her curvy body was dressed in a long black jacket and dark blue pants.

"Go away!" Naomi yelled. "I don't want to talk to you."

"Open up, Naomi. I want us to talk, please."

Naomi stood there for a moment, considering her options. After a moment, she decided to let Tanya in. She wondered what excuse Tanya would give for having sex with those girls that she had seen her with. Or was she going to lie about it?

"Thank you," Tanya said as she stepped inside, trying to make eye contact with Naomi's angry glare.

"Okay?" Naomi said when they got to her living room.

"I'm sorry about everything, Naomi," Tanya began, hugging her black jacket tighter around her chest. "We had something beautiful, and I didn't value it enough. But I do now. I know how much I have missed seeing you next to me or hearing your voice. I miss everything about you. You are a special girl, and you deserve all the attention in the world from the person you love. I'm sorry I could not do it, but I'm ready to fix things up. Give me a chance, please."

Naomi stared at Tanya for a moment, torn between giving her a chance because she had sounded reasonable when she spoke and telling her to leave because she needed to sleep.

"Why did you bang those girls?"

"Lack of control, lack of respect to the relationship, whatever you want to call it. I take responsibility, and I know it won't happen again. I guess I have insecurities too. I didn't know if you really wanted me or if it was just experimentation."

Naomi was unable to speak for a moment. She stared into Tanya's eyes as if trying to dig up any hidden meanings there.

"Okay," Naomi said. It felt too easy, she thought. Tanya had broken her heart, and here she was, taking her back so fast.

Naomi was still engrossed in thinking that she had given in to Tanya's pleas a little too easily.

"Wait here a second, okay?" Tanya said as she dashed back out to her car.

Naomi stared at the ceiling. She couldn't help that her heart felt happy, but she was also terrified of entering another of Tanya's games. Her trust was struggling to make amends. Her heart was muddled around.

Just let her talk.

"Here you go. I wanted to see if you'd let me in first," Tanya said as she handed over a bouquet of sweet-smelling fresh red roses.

"Wow, these are so beautiful," Naomi said as she took the bouquet from Tanya and held it to her nose, inhaling the fragrance.

"There's something even better," Tanya said.

"What's that?"

"I want you to be all mine, to be my darling alone," Tanya began. "Will you be mine forever? I don't have a ring here, but we can do that tomorrow. I just want a yes to my question."

Naomi was surprised by the suddenness of Tanya's proposal. "Let's still go out with each other for a bit longer. Don't you think? We don't want..."

She stopped short when she noticed the way Tanya was staring at her lips. At that moment, she felt the urge to hug Tanya and lock lips with her, as they had always done. Naomi wasn't sure who made the first move, but in a blink, she was kissing Tanya and running her hands up and down her body. A wave of passion ran through Naomi's body as she moved her lips against Tanya's. It was clear that they had missed each other. Naomi thought she found more comfort than ever within Tanya's passionate embrace.

Tanya broke their kiss for a moment while she kept

her hand on Naomi's neck. "I don't know if I have ever told you this, Naomi. I love you."

Naomi opened her mouth to say she loved Tanya, too, but she took a moment to weigh her feelings. She accepted that it was the truth. That this woman had changed her heart and made her realize what true love really was and how painful it was to almost lose it.

"Yeah, I love you, too, but don't fuck me around again?" Naomi replied, and they sealed that declaration with another round of passionate kissing.

"I'm sorry. I know I have to work to deal with my own issues, but I've never cared so much for any girl," Tanya said after breaking their kiss. "I feel as if I've been waiting my entire life to find you. It all makes sense now. What do you think about moving in with me?" Tanya asked her.

Naomi could not believe her ears. She was too surprised to give an immediate response. She could only marvel at how things had gone from terrible to fantastic in the space of only a few minutes. If she had dreamed up any of these things happening, she would have thought it was too unrealistic. Eager to have another taste of Tanya's lips, Naomi leaned forward to resume their kiss. They held each other in the dimly lit living room, enjoying the moment.

"I missed you. I missed the taste of your lips," Tanya moaned.

"I missed you tasting me. Nobody has ever made me as excited as you," Naomi replied as she felt her clit tingling every time Tanya kissed her. "I want you to touch me."

Tanya smiled mid-kiss as she slipped her hand underneath Naomi's nightshirt, discovering she was not wearing any panties. She slid her hand between Naomi's thighs, rubbing her fingers around her wetness, teasing her hot opening. Naomi's clit started to swell with excitement, showing how Tanya's love and passion thrilled her, sending a throbbing sensation throughout her core.

"It's crazy the way you make me feel. I shouldn't forgive you so easily when you hurt me, but I can't help myself."

Tanya stopped for a moment to reply, "I promise to explain properly tomorrow, but it truly meant nothing. It was a silly fling with someone I've had brief flings with in the past. I was scared of commitment, and I was being self-destructive. I regretted it so much, Naomi."

"Okay, I believe you. I just want to say it again... I love you." Naomi replied as she spread her legs a little wider.

Tanya bit her lip and started to push her fingers inside Naomi as she draped her leg over the side of the chair for easier access. Naomi moaned as her face flushed red. Tanya filled her and started to fuck her harder into the chair before moving to take off her clothes and get down on her knees.

"I want to taste you properly," Tanya whispered as she tossed her clothes aside, and Naomi spread her legs open.

"I'm all yours, Tanya."

Tanya lapped at her wetness and started to suckle on Naomi's swollen clit as she pushed her fingers deep inside, fucking her deeply and slowly, gradually picking up the pace. Naomi fell back into the chair, enjoying every thrust. Tanya sucked on her clit hard, nibbling gently before flicking her tongue over her most sensitive part. Her fingers continued banging away at Naomi's hot core.

"I'm cumming, I'm going to cum so hard for you," Naomi moaned as her body tensed and her legs began to shake.

Tanya slowed down the thrusting, still staying inside of her. It was exciting how much she turned Naomi on and vice versa. She could make her cum in no time, and she wanted to do it over and over and over again.

"I love fucking you," Tanya said with a smirk on her face.

"I fucking love it too," Naomi replied as she looked down and grinned at Tanya, reaching for her hand.

"Come up here and kiss me, and in response to your earlier question, it would be pretty fun to spend more time together."

"I guess I need to give you back the spare key, honey," Tanya replied as she kissed Naomi and felt butterflies of happiness across her torso for the first time in her entire life.

EPILOGUE

I really hope you enjoyed this book! To get the epilogue for Lost in Desire featuring a hot sex scene (for free) click the link below.

HTTPS://BOOKHIP.COM/HKJHWXD

YOU WILL BE ASKED to sign up to my mailing list, but there is no obligation to stay if you change your mind.

THANK YOU SO MUCH,
Grace x

THANK YOU!

Thank you for reading my books. I really do hope that you enjoyed it! I would be grateful if you could spare a moment to leave a review on Amazon – they really do make a difference for Indie authors like myself.

Feel free to join my Lesfic Readers group on Facebook. If you search on Facebook for 'Grace Parkes LesFic Group' you'll find us there!

Please sign up to my mailing to be the first to know about my new releases! You'll also receive monthly free stuff as a little thank you:

https://mailchi.mp/2a09276da35f/graceparkeswrites

If you'd like to get in touch or keep up to date with what I'm up to, here's where to find me!

Twitter: https://www.twitter.com/GraceParkesFic

Facebook: https://www.facebook.com/graceparkesauthor

Email: graceparkeswrites@hotmail.com

Instagram: @graceparkeswrites

Please check out my other books. They are all available to read for free on Kindle Unlimited.

Bittersweet She

Tasha Robinson thought her average life would never change. For years Tasha had continued to stay in the same job, town and stale relationship – none of which brought excitement into her life.

As societal pressures smother Tasha, a weekend away with her best friend changes everything, but has it changed for the better?

Tasha meets a captivating girl who takes her breath away and is forced to make some difficult decisions which could potentially change her life forever.

Get it here: getbook.at/BittersweetShe

Her Secret

Sarah and Emily had everything they ever wanted, except a happy relationship.

After new girl Megan Jenkinson started working alongside Sarah, life began to change.

They embark on a heated affair which takes them both by surprise, especially Megan who had always been into guys.

Lies and deceit take everyone on a gripping adventure throughout this new steamy lesfic by exciting author Grace Parkes.

Disclaimer - this book contains cheating please don't read if you do not like this topic
Get it here: mybook.to/hersecretlesfic

The Business of Pleasure
Zora is an icon in the vibrant city of Aperth. Her guarded heart and busy lifestyle leave her with no time to think about any romantic involvement with women. Intrigued by the services offered by glamorous city girl Isabella, Zora is keen to know more. Life changes quickly is this hearty romance.

Rivalry in the city puts Zora's safety at risk, will fear force her to confront what is important to her?

Can Isabella break into Zora's frosty heart, or is there too much on the line including Isabella's safety?

Get it here: https://getbook.at/thebusinessofpleasure

Guitar Girl
Ava Sierra knew from a young age that she was destined for the stage. What she didn't know was the turbulent drama that was on its way into her life.

As she battles it out for the chance to break through into the music industry with her rebellious band, she collides with rival Charlotte Thunder who seems all too familiar.

Loud music, unrequited love and an unexpected chain of events will keep you turning pages in this new exciting lesfic by budding author Grace Parkes.

Get it here: getbook.at/GuitarGirl

Please Mistress

Fiona can't wait to leave her dysfunctional family life, her safe boyfriend and the small town she grew up in far behind her when she goes to Music School in the city.

She needs to figure out what she wants in life and love, but there seem to be more questions than answers.

Then there is her growing obsession with her aloof singing teacher, Joss Red.

Will Fiona find a way to tell Joss about her fantasies?

Get it here: http://getbook.at/pleasemistress

Before Her

Cara Taylor has spent her life in a small village without much excitement. She works in a bar, lives with her best friend and without realising is in need of something new and exciting.

After meeting her best friend's new tenant Frankie, she is desperate to find out more.

Can Cara break down Frankie's barriers and find love in the land that time forgot?

Get it here: My Book

Code of Conduct

Victoria is used to being in charge, but her own values are pushed when she has to mentor her new and eager student nurse, Ella.

Passion takes her by surprise, putting her career on the line.

Will Victoria adhere to The Code of Conduct or risk it all for Ella?

Get it here: My Book

Once again, thank you x